MW00886755

## Prologue

When Chad Meyers and Jeremy Butcher bought the old Sherriff's office building in 1988 for $1,000, they had no idea what they were going to do with the building. But barely legally able to sign a legally binding contract at the time, Chad, then 18 and Jeremy, then 19 knew it was what they had to do, and knew that, even in 1988, $1,000 for a building like this was a steal. The county had plans to demolish the old building because they considered it blight, sitting empty in a part of town with little around it, if it didn't find a buyer, and neither Chad nor Jeremy wanted to see that happen.

The building was a yellow brick, one-story building with ceilings that were probably 20 feet tall. From the outside, the building had the appearance of a two-story building, but the upper windows, long ago painted shut, were there to allow air to flow into and out of the building in the days before air conditioning, and were opened and closed with a long, darkly-stained wooden pole, slightly wider than a broom stick, with a hook on the end, and, facing east, the windows still allowed rays of sunshine that looked like masses of sparkling guitar strings, to shine into the building.

Chad and Jeremy's fathers had been best friends since grade school, and when their fathers married their mothers, the two families, with one child each, became fast friends, living just a block from each other. Being just a year apart, Chad and Jeremy grew up almost like brothers.

Both sets of parents encouraged the purchase of the building, and each lent their son $500 toward the purchase price.

The building sat empty for a few years, and not knowing what to do with the building, Chad's father suggested turning it into a restaurant.

"You and Jeremy have both worked at McDonalds for a few months, so you know how to cook. Your mom makes an awesome Thousand Island dressing with red pepper relish. I make some mean barbecue ribs, and Mrs. Butcher has a great spinach and artichoke dip recipe. I think you have everything it takes to open a restaurant. You could call it Chad & Jeremy's Place."

Chad and Jeremy's dads went to Price Club and bought all the supplies and ingredients they thought they would need to open a restaurant, borrowing 30 pressboard fold-up tables and 200 chairs from the local rotary club. Mrs. Meyers typed out menus on her Selectric typewriter, making three carbon copies of each menu she typed, tiring after typing seven menus and figuring twenty-eight menus would be enough.

Inexperienced and not realizing that the best way to open a restaurant is quietly, with no press, and little advertising in the middle of the week, Chad and Jeremy opened "Visit Bubba in Prison" on Sunday, May 12, 1991 to great fanfare. Neither liked the idea of using their own names as part of the restaurant's name, and decided that because, even though the building had been a Sherriff's Office and not a prison, it had a few jail cells in the back, they would incorporate something about the jail cells into the restaurant's name. Neither one can remember where the name Bubba came from, but Jeremy later said "it just sounded like a prisoner's name." Although it had a jail and not a prison, they thought the word prison made a more lasting impression. They took out full page ads in the Rustfield Register, bought radio ads on several local radio stations, all of which said "Come to Visit Bubba in Prison," and told all their friends, and told their friends to tell all of their friends.

Needless to say opening on Mother's Day was a train wreck. They had three servers, no host, and Chad and Jeremy were doing all of the cooking. Their dads jumped in to help cook. Their moms came in and acted as hostesses, but the crowd was overwhelming, the restaurant was running out of food, and the food that was coming out of the kitchen was taking two hours or more to come out. The six of them and their staff were deflated and beaten.

Despite opening day, the restaurant opened on time the next day, with the two dads making a run to Price Club to replenish, well, everything. The second day went more smoothly, either because almost nobody wanted to come because they had such a bad experience the previous day, or because it was a Monday, or possibly both. The second day went much smoother.

Fortunately, the public was forgiving, and by 1994, the little restaurant in the middle of nowhere was a destination. The food was good but not gourmet, but people liked the atmosphere, and people liked telling their friends "We're going to Visit Bubba in Prison." By this time, the two jail cells, which initially each had a life-sized replica of a man in a prison outfit in the middle of the cell, were more than just for display. Each cell had three tables in it, the replicas of the prisoners named Bubba had been moved to the corners of the jail cells, and people would ask to eat in prison.

But again there were problems. There was talk in the county of demolishing the building, this time, not because it was considered blight, but because a developer, ACA Development Company wanted to build a mall on the site. Chad and Jeremy were not sure where to turn to save their restaurant. Sure they could move, but what building would have the same character of this building? They could move the building, but that would cost hundreds of thousands of dollars and mean being closed for weeks or months.

Fortunately Chad and Jeremy had to do nothing. A 60-year old woman named Adelaide Whitford who had lived in town her whole life started a grassroots effort to save the building. She collected signatures, rallied people to protest in front of ACA's office, and even scheduled several meetings with the mayor and the city planning commission. Neither Chad nor Jeremy knew Adelaide at the time, and neither knew if she started her campaign because she liked their restaurant, wanted to save an old building, or both, but neither cared.

By late 1994, a compromise was reached, and both the city planning commission and ACA Development Company agreed that instead of demolishing the old building, the mall would be built around the building, opening up the right side of the building with three large sliding glass doors, and adding eight more tables to the restaurant on the other side of the sliding glass doors in the new mall, cordoned off by a wrought iron railing.

Adelaide became a daily fixture in the restaurant, drinking her Shirley Temple, the old-fashioned way of course, with ginger ale and grenadine, garnished with a maraschino cherry, and eating her Chef Salad with Mrs. Meyer's signature Thousand Island dressing.

When Adelaide died in 2017, they dedicated a corner of the restaurant, Adelaide's Corner, to her, with a plaque, and a few articles about her successful efforts to save their restaurant almost a quarter of a century before, and changed the name of their Chef Salad to Adelaide's Chef Salad. "We wouldn't be here without her." Jeremy said in a 2017 interview with the Rustfield Register. "Literally," he added, choking up.

# Server Test for Visit Bubba In Prison
## You MUST pass with a 90% score before your first shift.

What THREE questions do you ask a guest who orders one of Bubba's 1/3 pound burgers?

Which type of bread is NOT offered at Bubba's?
- ☐ Pumpernickel
- ☐ Rye
- ☐ Sourdough
- ☐ Brioche Bun

Which sandwich DOES NOT come with sauerkraut?
- ☐ The Reuben Sandwich
- ☐ The Roast Beef Sandwich
- ☐ The Pastrami Sandwich
- ☐ You're being silly. All our sandwiches come with sauerkraut

What makes Mrs. Meyer's Special Thousand Island Dressing unique from most other Thousand Island dressings?

In your own words, how would you describe Morbier cheese to a guest?

What THREE types of mushrooms are on the Cremini Salad?

List the ingredients on Adelaide's Chef Salad?

What do you say to a guest who orders wings but wants all flats or all drums?

What would you suggest to a guest who tells you they are thinking of the Fiery Prawns and Pasta but that they don't like spicy food?

Which of Bubba's sandwiches can a guest order with the Lunch Combo?

Why are we not able to accommodate the request for a Lunch Combo after 4 PM or on the weekends?

A guest tells you they don't eat pork. Which item would you NOT suggest to this guest?
- ☐ The Reuben Sandwich
- ☐ Meatloaf
- ☐ Basic Pomodoro Pasta
- ☐ Raspberry Limeade

What two sizes of pizza does Bubba's offer for our thin and crispy pizzas?

What do you tell a guest who orders a deep dish pizza?

Which item do we serve each day until we run out?

Why is it important to suggest a drink and an appetizer by name?

How many slices of banana are on Bubba's I'll Regret It But Duck It I'm Gonna Get it Banana Split?

What are Bubba's THREE signature wines?

What should be left on a table after you pre-bus a table?

Who must approve all schedule changes?

# Menu

### Beginnings

**Cheasy to Eat Cheese Bread** – Our signature bread topped with melted Mozzarella, Parmesan, and Morbier cheeses. $9

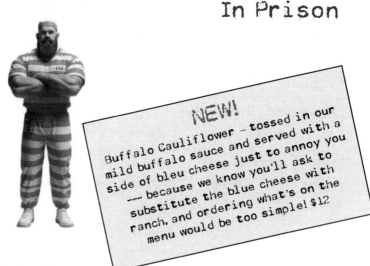

**NEW!**
Buffalo Cauliflower – tossed in our mild buffalo sauce and served with a side of bleu cheese just to annoy you --- because we know you'll ask to substitute the blue cheese with ranch, and ordering what's on the menu would be too simple! $12

**Mrs. Butcher's Spinach and Artichoke Dip** – Spinach and Artichokes mixed with Mozzarella, Parmesan, and Morbier cheeses. $11

**Gotcha Nachos** –A huge plate of nachos, topped with, Mozzarella, Parmesan, and Morbier cheeses, and any of our pizza toppings you'd like. What? You're going to ask your server what you can put on your nachos because you're too lazy to turn the page to look at the list? $11

**Cheese Twigs** – Strips of batter and fried Morbier cheese, served with Mrs. Meyer's Signature 1000 island dressing --- we dare you to try it without a side of ranch! $10

**Wings** – Ten wings served with celery & carrot sticks and your choice of ranch or bleu cheese. $16

### Things Mixed with Lettuce

**The Carnegie Salad** - black olives, green peppers, capers, tomatoes, cucumbers, hard-boiled egg, carrots, mushrooms and cheddar cheese, served with Mrs. Meyer's Special Thousand Island Dressing. $12

**The Cremini Salad** – for the mushroom lover in you! A bed of lettuce topped with cremini mushrooms, but we don't stop there --- we've added portabellas, oyster mushrooms, and shiitakes for a mouthwatering experience you're sure to enjoy. $13

**Adelaide's Chef Salad** – Turkey, Bacon, Ham, hard-boiled egg, shredded Morbier and Cheddar Cheeses served with Mrs. Meyer's Special Thousand Island Dressing, and a complimentary Shirley Temple, if you order it with ginger ale. $14

**Crispy Chicken Salad** – Crispy chicken, cheddar cheese, provolone cheese, mozzarella cheese, cherry tomatoes, and carrots on a bed of greens, served with our warm mustardy bacon dressing. $14

Chicken Salad Platter – Served on a bed of lettuce with tomatoes, black olives, cucumbers, and potato salad or coleslaw. $14

Tuna Salad Platter – Served on a bed of lettuce with tomatoes, black olives, cucumbers, and potato salad or coleslaw. $14

## Chunks of Cows and Pigs

Meatloaf – Mrs. Butcher's special mix of pork, beef, and secret spices, wrapped in bacon and smothered with our own Pomodoro sauce – served with a baked potato, mashed potatoes, or fries. Substitute potato salad or coleslaw at no extra charge if you say please. $18

8 ounce Sirloin – served with a baked potato, mashed potatoes, or fries. Substitute potato salad or coleslaw at no extra charge if you say please. $18

12 Ounce Prime Rib – served with Au Jus, a baked potato, mashed potatoes, or fries. Substitute potato salad or coleslaw at no extra charge if you say please. $18

22 ounce Porterhouse – served with a baked potato, mashed potatoes, or fries. Substitute potato salad or coleslaw at no extra charge if you say please. $36

Mr. Meyers' Mean Barbecue Ribs – A full rack of our slow roasted and served with signature barbecue sauce – served with a baked potato, mashed potatoes, or fries. Substitute potato salad or coleslaw at no extra charge if you say please. Served each day until we run out. $16

Surf and turf – Served with your choice of steak, price varies, of course, and a baked potato, mashed potatoes, or fries. Substitute potato salad or coleslaw at no extra charge if you say please.

## Things Made with Flour, Water, and Eggs

Basic Pomodoro Pasta – Your choice of spaghetti, fettucine, Cavatappi, or bowtie noodles served with Pomodoro Sauce. $14

Fiery Prawns and Pasta – 8 huge prawns served on fettucine with our fiery sauce. $18

Sweet and Sour Shrimp with Pasta – 8 huge prawns served on fettucine with our sweet and sour sauce. $18

## Things on Round Bread Made with Red Sauce

Thin and crispy or deep dish • 16 inches or 20 inches for our thin pizzas • 14 inches for our deep dish pizzas $18, $22, $26.

## Toppings:
Pepperoni • Sausage • Ground beef • Mushrooms • Bacon • Extra cheese • Onion • Black olives • Green pepper• Fresh garlic • Tomato • Spinach • Fresh basil • Artichokes • Pickles • Pineapple • Fresh mozzarella • Eggplant • Pepperoncini $3 for deep dish and 16 inch, $4 for 20 inch.

## Things Served on Bread

The Reuben Sandwich – Corned Beef and Sauerkraut topped with Morbier cheese, with our spicy mustard. Served on your choice of bread and our fries. $12

The Pastrami Sandwich – Pastrami and Sauerkraut topped with Morbier cheese, with our spicy mustard. Served on your choice of bread and our fries. $12

The Grilled Cheese Sandwich – Served on your choice of bread and with your choice of Morbier, Swiss or American cheese and our fries. $10

The TLB – our version of the BLT, made with thick cut pig belly, lettuce, and tomato, on your choice of bread, served with our fries. $12

Tuna Salad Sandwich – Served on your choice of bread with our fries. $12

Chicken Salad Sandwich – Served on your choice of bread with our fries. $12

Burgers – 1/3 pound of ground cow served. Add any or our pizza toppings to your burger, or get it plain, served with our fries. Not a math whiz? It's bigger than their 1/4 burger... trust us! $16

Filet of Fish – Served with your choice of Remoulade Sauce or Tartar Sauce on a brioche bun with melted American cheese and our fries. $14

The Roast Beef Sandwich – Served with Au Jus on a brioche bun with melted Morbier cheese and our fries. $16

The Prime Rib Sandwich – Served with Au Jus on a brioche bun with melted Morbier cheese and our fries. $18

## For The Young Uns

Chicken Toes – Served with French Fries and ranch dressing. Real toes? We'll never tell! $8

Kid's Hot Dog – Served with French Fries and ranch dressing. Not sure what's in it? Neither are we, but we CAN guarantee you no dogs were harmed in the making of our hot dog. $8

Kid's Pasta – Your choice of pasta with Pomodoro sauce. Don't like Pomodoro sauce? Too bad, you're just a kid. Sit down, shut up, pretend you like it and eat it. Just kidding. We'll substitute any sauce you want. $6

Mac 'N Cheese – Our own blend of Mozzarella, Parmesan, and Morbier cheeses, with a little bit of yellow food coloring so it looks just like the stuff that comes out of a box. $6

## Diet Killers

Duck My Diet I'll Try It Chocolate Cake – The best chocolate cake you'll ever have! $8

I'll Regret It But Duck It I'm Gonna Get it Banana Split – Our signature banana split, made with 3 slices of banana! $8

Ice Cream Mundae – Ice cream, hot fudge, nuts, whipped cream and a cherry! $8

Go ahead and have one. You weren't really on a diet anyway. Who're you kidding?

## Lunch --- Served Monday through Friday until 4 P.M.

Your choice of half of any of our sandwiches served with our signature vegetable soup, the soup of the day, or a small salad. Want a lunch combo on the weekend or after 4 P.M. Just ask your server. They'll say no, but go ahead and ask anyway. $11

## Wet Things

Raspberry Limeade – A bunch of purple and green chemicals mixed together to make you think it tastes like raspberries and limes. $5
Blueberry Orangeade – A bunch of blue and orange chemicals mixed together to make you think it tastes like blueberries and oranges. $5
Guava Lemonade – Guava mixed with fresh lemonade, dispensed FRESH from our soda gun. Don't know what guava is? That's okay, neither do we. Don't google it. Just try it. $5

Prisoner Red Blend $17 / $65
Prisoner Cabernet Sauvignon $17 / $65
Prisoner Chardonnay $17 / $65

Coke, Diet Coke, Sprite, Fanta Orange, Dr. Pepper, and Lemonade $3.5
Free refills if you say please.

Side of Ranch:

$.99 if ordered when you order your meal.
$1.99 if ordered when your server brings your food out to the table.

$1.49 charge for extra cheese *** $1.99 charge for extra sauerkraut.

Join Bubba's Prison Inmate Gang and get a FREE dessert for your birthday. Ask your server for details.

Allergy Warning: Some menu items may contain or come into contact with wheat, eggs, nuts and milk. Ask our staff for more information.

Suggested gratuity of 20% added for parties of 6 or more.

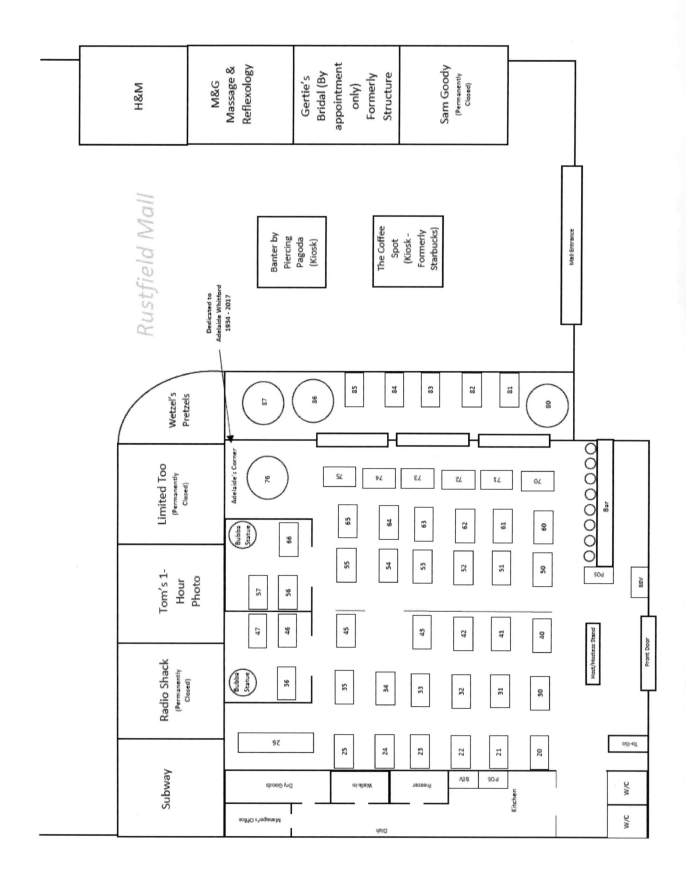

Rustfield Mall

Milo was excited about his new job at the restaurant, Visit Bubba in Prison. Although it was an odd name for a restaurant, he thought nothing of it. After all, his parents took him there as kid, first eating the kid's chicken toes, throwing most of them along with his fries, on his booster seat or the floor, and later eating the 8 ounce sirloin, none of which ended up on the floor. And, of course he remembered having his picture taken, many times, with one of two life-sized replicas of a prisoner named Bubba in a prison cell.

Now Milo would have some money of his own, and after all, it's a restaurant. You bring people their food. How hard could it be?

Milo, a slightly smaller than average sized guy, about 5' 9" with dirty blond hair, had lived a somewhat sheltered life and had not had many life experiences.

As he filled out his new-hire paperwork at what he would later learn was table 20, he heard the server greet a couple of women, one with a distinct accent that he couldn't place, but even at his young age, knew reeked of privilege, or at very least entitlement. Before the server could even greet the table, the woman started talking.

"I'll have the bacon cheeseburger," the lady with the distinct accent said. Milo thought "wow," that was easy! "I'm going to love this job."

"But" the lady continued on. "I want the burger slightly charred on the outside, but not burnt, and pink in the middle. Make sure you tell the chef I want it pink, and not red. Make sure the burger is hot. If it's cold I'm sending it back. "But," she continued, "I want the tomatoes, lettuce and pickles nice and cold. Make sure you tell the chef. And I want the fries hot. I don't want fries that have been sitting around waiting for my burger to cook. They need to come out of the fryer at the same time my burger is done cooking."

"I'll just have the cook put the tomatoes, lettuce and pickles on the side. That way they'll stay cold," the server said.

"No," the lady chirped emphatically. "I want them ON my burger. I just want them cold."

Even without experience, Milo could tell the server was beginning to get frustrated with the woman.

"Okay," the server said. "And what do you want to drink?"

"Oh yes," the woman said indignantly. "You forgot to get my drink order."

Although Milo couldn't see the server behind him, he imagined her metaphorically rolling eyes.

"I'll have an RC Cola," the woman said. "But bring it WITH the food."

"We have Coke products," the server said to the woman.

Faking exasperation, the woman simply replied "Okay, I guess that'll have to do," as if she was making a sacrifice. "But bring it WITH my food."

Milo wondered, if they even made RC Cola anymore, and IF someone gave the woman a glass of RC Cola and glass of Coca Cola, without telling her which was which, she would even know the difference. He had heard of RC Cola, but never tasted it. Now he started to wonder what it tasted like.

Milo began to fill out his W-4 when he heard the second woman speak up, and realized that after all this time, the server, who he would later learn was named Sandy and had been at the restaurant for about 10 years, had not gotten the chance to get the other woman's order.

"I'll have a Coke," the other woman said, "and whenever you want to bring it is fine. And I'll just have the tuna platter."

"That comes with a choice of potato salad or coleslaw," Sandy said.

Before the woman could answer, the woman who ordered the burger chimed in. "Is the potato salad made fresh in the restaurant?" Milo wondered why the woman who ordered the burger cared so much about the freshness of the other woman's side dish, but before Sandy could answer, the woman who was going to be eating the potato salad, whether it was fresh or scooped out of a 1-gallon tub from Costco, or the coleslaw, replied.

"Surprise me."

Milo also wondered why the other woman had asked whether the potato salad was made fresh but didn't ask whether the coleslaw was made fresh.

"But if that's all there is to it, this job is going to be easy," Milo thought to himself.

***

When Milo was done with his paperwork, Victor, who was probably in his early 30s but appeared a little older, had greying, uncombed hair and a thick moustache, and often wore a grey or beige huckapoo shirt and polyester pants, came and collected it. "I'll give this to Andy when he gets in."

"Andy?" Milo asked.

"Andy is the GM," Victor replied. "He takes care of inputting your information into the system."

"GM," Milo thought. "Good Moring? General Motors?" Milo didn't understand what it meant, but he didn't want to seem to naïve, so he just said okay.

"This is Sandy," Victor said to Milo as Sandy, a shorter woman, with curly greying hair and Boston accent, approached carrying a stack of dishes. "Sandy is going to be training you."

Milo felt as if he already knew Sandy, but simply said "nice to meet you," as she walked by without stopping. A few minutes later Sandy came back, sans dishes and said "Okay, let me give you a tour of the restaurant."

As they walked, Sandy began to talk. "The table numbers all go in rows, and start with 20, 30, 40 etc. This is table 20," Sandy said pointing to the table where Milo had filled out his new-hire paperwork, and began pointing at each subsequent table "and 21, 22, 23, and so on. You simply count beginning with the lowest number to figure out the table numbers. Except for table 44. There is no table 44 because they took it out when they cut that doorway in," pointing to a doorway in a half-wall between two tables.

"And this is the prison," Sandy said as they got to the back of the restaurant and pointed to two rooms that looked like jail cells, with bars, doors, and locks, with the doors chained and padlocked in the open position. This building used to be the county Sherriff's office, and these were the jail cells where they held people overnight, until they could transport them somewhere else or release them. The tables in this one," as she pointed to the left cell, "are 36, 46 and 47, and the tables in this one," as she pointed to the right cell, "are 56, 57 and 66. People love to sit at these tables. Sometimes we push them together for large parties. People love to use the bars for photo ops, and they love to have their picture taken with Bubba," pointing to both replicas of Bubba.

Milo quickly reminisced about having his picture taken with Bubba as a kid, but his mind quickly snapped back to reality. "Whose section it that?" he asked innocently, thinking maybe servers were permanently assigned to sections.

"We don't usually assign it," Sandy said. "Usually one of the servers in a section nearby will pick it up when it gets seated, because you need to be a stronger server to handle the larger parties, and the stronger servers usually have the sections in the back of the restaurant, because that is where most people want to sit since it's farther away from the door."

As they walked toward the right side of the restaurant, they passed a row of hi-tops. "And these are the 70s," Sandy said. "The bartender usually takes these tables, but on a busy night, a server might have them." They walked a few more feet, and Sandy pushed open one of three heavy sliding glass doors. "And this is The Mall," as she pointed to an area that had eight more tables, and was cordoned off from the mall with a wrought iron railing that Milo guessed to be about three or four feet tall.

"They wanted to tear this building down when they built the mall back in '94, but the community objected, so they built the mall around the building and incorporated the building into the mall. When I started here, everyone wanted to sit out here. I guess they wanted to sit here because they could watch people in the mall. Now, with only a handful of stores left in the mall, it's kind of depressing out here, and no one wants to sit here. We only seat people out here if they ask, or if we have a large party."

As they approached the bar area Sandy began again. "This is the service bar, she said, pointing to an area next to the bar. This is where you pick up your drinks, and there is a soda station right next to it. This is the server station, with cups, ice, straws, stuff like that, and this is our POS. It's called Aloha. I'll train you on that as we go. There are two terminals here, two terminals in the kitchen, oh, and we have an identical server station in the kitchen, and one terminal at the to-go station. Try not to use the terminal at the to-go station when it's busy."

"If it's so bad, why do they keep it?" Milo asked innocently, thinking POS meant piece of shit.

Not catching on to Milo's interpretation of the acronym, Sandy continued. "It's really not bad. I kind of like it."

"And this is Bubba, or I should say, the Bubbas," she continued, pointing to a row of about 15 prisoner figurines in prison garbs, about one foot high, mounted on a base, all slightly different from each other.

Some had black and white stripes on their prison outfit. Some had orange and white stripes. Some had a full beard while others just had a 1970s porn star moustache. Some were holding a pick axe and others had a ball and chain around one ankle while still others had both ankles shackled together.

"There are more of them at the server station in the kitchen. We used to grab one and grab enough silverware for each person at the table, and put it on the table. That is the signal to everyone else who works here that the table has been greeted, but people really don't remember to grab them and put them on the tables anymore, so they rarely get used. They are silent when they are sitting on the base here at the service bar but once they get to a table, they spew funny lines periodically, such as this 'This prison food is terrible.' Guests love them but they can silence them by pushing this little button here," and she pointed to a button on the bottom of the base with the word 'silence' on it.

"What happens if someone tries to steal one?" Milo asked.

"They're kind of big to steal," Sandy said, "but let's find out. Grab one."

Milo grabbed the closest Bubba to him, and he and Sandy headed to the front door of the restaurant, opened the door, and walked out, Bubba in hand. "Prison break, Prison break," Bubba screamed.

"Let's go back in and try it again," Sandy said.

The two went back in to the restaurant and went back out again.

"I'm free, I'm free," Bubba yelled this time.

***

Days one and two of Milo's training went well, or pretty well to put it nicely. The first day, Milo just shadowed Sandy and listened and observed. On day two Sandy had Milo begin to practice helping out.

Soon after the restaurant opened on day two of Milo's training, Sandy got a 10-top, and she engaged Milo to help out.

"Hi," Sandy said. "My name is Sandy, and I'll be taking care of you today. And this is Milo. He's training with me today."

"Hi Milo," almost everyone said in harmony, as if Milo was new to a support group and being introduced at his first group meeting, but completely not acknowledging Sandy.

"Can I start anyone with a drink?" Sandy asked. "Possibly a Long Island Iced Tea, or a Bloody Mary? A Raspberry Limeade or Blueberry Orangeade?"

"Do you have Coke or Pepsi products?" Someone asked.

"We have Coke products," Sandy Replied.

"I'll have a Coke," someone said.

"I'll also have a Coke," Someone else said. "And a water."

"I'll have a Sprite."

"Do you have Dr. Pepper?" Someone asked.

"We do," Sandy replied.

"I'll have a Dr. Pepper and a water."

When everyone had ordered, Sandy and Milo made their way over to the beverage station.

"Okay," Sandy said, "I don't usually give people water unless they ask because they are less likely to order a beverage if they have water. But since a few people asked for water, let's just get them all a water, because if you only bring water for the people who asked for it, the others will ask for water too when they see it. It'll save you a trip. Always consolidate your steps. I'll make the sodas, and you make ten waters."

Milo finished making the waters before Sandy finished making the sodas. "Can I bring them over to the table" Milo asked.

"Sure," Sandy said.

A little shaky, Milo headed back to the table with ten waters on a tray, his right hand under the tray and his left hand holding the side of the tray. As he got to the table, Milo started to take the waters off the tray, changing the placement of his hand under the tray as he took each water off, and distributed them to the guests. He tenaciously got four waters off of the tray and distributed them to the guests as he moved around the table.

Sensing that he was having trouble balancing the tray, one of the guests turned around. "Here, let me help you hun," she said, as she grabbed the two waters nearest to her from the tray."

As she grabbed the two waters, Milo felt what seemed like a cold wave hit him as the tray fell backwards, the remaining four waters falling back toward Milo and onto his shirt and jeans, and then falling to the floor, cups, tray and all.

"I am SOOOO sorry," the lady said to Milo, who was still in shock trying to grasp what happened.

"It's uh, it's uh, alright," Milo said, dusting his wet shirt of the way you would dust flour or dirt, but to no avail.

"It's okay," Sandy said, as she approached with the tray of sodas, setting them down on the next table. "Go dry yourself off and see if Victor will give you another shirt, and I'll get this cleaned up."

"Clean up on aisle two," was playing in Milo's head, the way they announce on the PA system in a grocery store, as he walked toward the office, leaving a trail of water behind him. "I guess they don't make that announcement in restaurants," he thought to himself.

*** 

"I'll have my 12 ounce ribeye well done," the older man with the hat said.

"And what side would you like with that?" Milo asked. By this point Milo had progressed enough in his training that Sandy was letting him take a few tables while she shadowed him. This man and his friend had chatted for 20 minutes before even looking at the menu, so Sandy figured this would be a good table for Milo to take, since they did not appear to be famished or in a hurry.

"I'll have the baked potato," the man said, quickly adding "Without the butter. My doctor says I have to watch my cholesterol." Milo wasn't sure if the man who had just ordered a 12 ounce steak was joking about watching his cholesterol, but he kept his mouth shut, and wrote it down.

"I'll have exactly what he's having," the other man said to Milo. "But I'll have butter on my baked potato. My doctor told me to watch my cholesterol too, so I need a little extra cholesterol to watch," the man joked, as if it was supposed to be funny.

As he and Sandy turned to leave the table, Milo noticed that the next table was just being seated. Remembering Sandy's talk about consolidating his steps, Milo stopped at that table to welcome the lady who had just been seated, offer her a drink, and to let her know he'd be right back with her drink. Before he could say anything the lady said "Water with lemon. And I'm ready to order. I'm in a little bit of a hurry."

"Okay," Milo thought. "Nice to meet you too." Instead, he simply said "Sure! What would you like?"

"I'll have the chicken salad platter," the lady said.

Milo knew this was great item for someone in a hurry because he had just sold one, and during the busier times the kitchen sandbagged them, so all they had to do was pull them out of the refrigerator, put on some chopped parsley, and put them in the window.

"I'll be right back with your water," Milo said, and he and Sandy walked toward the POS.

"Okay, let me put that lady's order in first since she is in a hurry, and the other table seems to be taking their time" Milo said to Sandy.

"No," Sandy said. "Great thinking, but because the chicken salad platters are premade, she may figure that out if it comes up too quickly. You want it to come up fast, but not too fast. Put the other order in first."

\*\*\*

"Oh, this salad looks good," Milo heard the lady saying to the gentleman with her as he approached the table.

"Hi. My name…"

"I think I'll have this Carnegie Salad," the lady interrupted. "It looks delicious."

Milo abandoned his greeting and wrote it down.

"But," the lady said, "I don't want any black olives, green peppers, capers, tomatoes, cucumbers or egg. Oh, and I don't want any cheese either. And what is this Mrs. Meyer's dressing that comes with it?"

"It's our version of a Thousand Island Dressing," Milo Replied "It's made with a red pepper relish instead of pickle relish. Other than ranch, it's our most popular dressing."

"Oh no," the lady replied. "I can't have that. Just bring me some oil and vinegar on the side. And I'll have a Coke. But bring it with my food."

Milo turned to the man with her. "And what would you like?" he asked.

"How's the Reuben sandwich?" the man asked.

In just a few short days at the restaurant, Milo had already come to hate this question almost as much as he hated when someone asked him "What's good here?" or "What's your favorite sandwich?" He liked most of their sandwiches, but if he said "it's delicious," it sounds canned like he just wants to affirm to the guest that they made the right choice, and although he really did like the Reuben, he wasn't going to throw one of their menu items under the bus.

"That's one of my favorite sandwiches," Milo said, thinking of some of the other sandwiches he also really liked.

"Well, the Prime Rib sandwich also sounds good," the man said.

"It is," Milo quickly replied, "But personally I prefer the Reuben Sandwich," proud of his diplomacy without throwing either sandwich under the bus.

"Okay," the man said. "I'll have the Reuben sandwich, but how sour is the sauerkraut?"

"Stanley!" The woman chimed in. "It's sauerkraut so it's sour. Don't be so difficult!" saying what Milo really wanted to say but couldn't, and then thinking about how specific she was with her order.

Leaving the table to go ring in the order, Milo noticed the couple at the next table had cash on the table. He stopped to take the cash, and remembering that Sandy had told him never to ask if the guest needed change, said "I'll be right back with your change," as he picked up the four twenty dollar bills the man had fanned out on the table.

"No, it's all yours," the man said, as they got up to leave.

"Thank you," Milo said. Not remembering how much their bill was, Milo walked over to the server station and looked at the amount of the check. $76.83. "Why do people feel they simply need to round up to the next even number when they tip?" he wondered.

Milo walked up to the table to greet the middle-aged couple that had just been seated. As he was greeting them, he saw through the corner of his eye that Dominic, the host was seating him again. Dominic appeared to Milo to be about his age, but slightly taller with short dark hair and a slim build.

"No problem," Milo thought. "I'll get them some drinks and go greet the new table."

"Hi," Milo said. "My name is Milo and I'll be taking care of you today. Can I start you with a Martini or a Bloody Mary while you're looking over the menu?" Milo found that by offering drinks that people rarely ordered, he often got a chuckle out of his guests, and loosened them up.

"We're ready to order everything," the man said. He sat for a few seconds and looked at the woman with him and said "Are you going to have a pasta?"

"I don't know," the woman said. "I was thinking of a sandwich."

"Because if you want to get a pasta, I'll get a pizza and we can share," the man said, "but I'm not in the mood for a sandwich."

"Yeah, I'll get a pasta," the woman said. "Which pasta sounds good to you?"

As the woman asked this question, Milo could see that Dominic was seating him another table.

"How about if I give you a minute to decide and I'll get your drinks?" Milo politely asked.

"No, we're ready," the man said.

"I'll take the Pomodoro Pasta with bowtie noodles," the woman said.

"What's Pomodoro?" the man asked, waiting for either the woman or Milo to answer.

Before he could reply, the woman chimed in. "It's red sauce like I make at home. Don't worry you'll like it."

Milo wrote down the woman's order, and turned and looked at the man, his anxiety building as he could see the new table Dominic had seated him now had their menus closed and at the end of the table, signaling that they were ready to order. He looked around to see if maybe someone could help him, but all he could see was Dominic at the host/hostess station blissfully ignorant of Milo's predicament, chatting with the to-go girl.

"How big is the 16" pizza?" the man asked Milo. Not sure quite how to answer, Milo put his server book on the table and gestured with his hands approximately a 16" inch circle, although for all he knew it could also be a 14" inch circle, or an 18" inch circle, but it seemed to satisfy the man.

"Okay," the man said. "I'll have that with, uhhh," he began to look over the menu again at the toppings, "ummm pepperoni, sausage and mushrooms."

"I don't like mushrooms," the woman replied.

"We can do half with no mushrooms," Milo told her.

"Do we have to pay for mushrooms on the whole thing if we only get mushrooms on half?" the woman asked.

"No, you only get charged for mushrooms on half," Milo told her, not sure if his answer was correct.

"Okay, let's do that," the woman said.

"Oh, and," the man said and paused and put his thumb and his index finger on his forehead as if that was going to help him remember what he was about to say. "Um, have them make that pizza well done. I don't like no soggy pizza."

"Okay. And to drink?" Milo was now trying to keep his sentences as short as possible.

"I'll have a Pepsi," the woman replied.

"We have Coke products," Milo said.

"Okay, I'll have a Coke," the woman said.

"I'll have a Mountain Dew," the man said.

"He just told you they have Coke products Einstein," the woman snapped at the man. Trying not to chuckle because she called him Einstein, Milo was glad she snapped at him because that is what he FELT like doing.

"I'll just have a water," the man said, as if Milo had somehow failed him.

As, Milo backed away from the table, hoping they didn't think of any other questions, he could see the second of the two tables Dominic had seated him gesturing him to come over.

"I'll be right with you," Milo said, hoping his tone of voice sounded polite, and turned and walked to the first of the two tables Dominic had seated him.

"Hi" Milo said. "Can I start you with something to drink?"

"We're ready to order," the woman said, "and we really are ready to order," she said as she smiled. Milo sensed that she was sympathetic and had heard him taking the order at the previous table. "We'll both have the lunch combo with the Roast Beef Sandwich and the vegetable soup," she said, "oh, and two waters."

Milo thanked them and debated whether to ring in the orders for these two tables first, or to greet the third table Dominic had seated him, but quickly decided to greet the third table because he saw them looking at him.

"Hi" Milo said forgoing his normal greeting in an effort to save some time. "Can I start you with something to drink?"

"I'll have a Coke," one woman said.

"I'll have a Sprite," the other woman said.

"We're in a little bit of a hurry," the first woman said.

"Okay, what would you like?" Milo asked.

"I'll have the grilled cheese sandwich," the first woman said, "but how is it cooked," she added.

"It's grilled," Milo said, quickly hoping she didn't think he was being snarky, but any unintended snark was lost on her and she was satisfied with the answer.

"And I'll have the tuna salad sandwich on rye," the second woman said "and we're in a little bit of a rush."

"Yeah, your friend literally just told me that," Milo thought to himself. Instead he thanked them and went to the POS to ring in the three orders.

"Which one do I put in first?" Milo wondered. He settled on the second table's order, because they both ordered the same item, and he could just ring in one item and hit repeat item. He rang in the lunch combo with the Roast Beef Sandwich and the vegetable soup, and he saw it appear on his screen. He then hit the "repeat item" button but nothing happened. Milo figured he didn't touch the screen hard enough, so he hit the "repeat item" button again and hit send.

He decided to ring in the third table's order since they were in a rush, and as he was ringing it in, he noticed a RUSH modifier on the screen that he had never seen before. "Perfect," he thought, and hit the RUSH modifier after each of their two items.

As he finished ringing in the first table's order, he realized he had not gotten the drinks for any of the last three tables. He saw Caroline bringing out his Carnegie Salad and Reuben Sandwich, and felt relieved because that was one less thing to worry about.

He went up to the host/hostess station and interrupted Dominic's conversation with the to-go girl whose name he didn't know, a cute, smaller girl about Milo's age, who Milo imagined to wear a short pleated skirt when not at work, and somehow managed to look magical, even in her work jeans and t-shirt.

"Can either of you make me some drinks?" Milo asked.

"Bro, wassup?" Dominic asked, in a tone of voice that Milo interpreted as meaning "why can't you fucking take care of your own tables? I'm trying to flirt."

"You fucking double sat me while I was at a table who discussed the entire menu, almost literally, while they held me hostage," Milo thought.

Before he could reply, and he was glad he couldn't, Caroline, a tall thin woman with straight, dirty blond shoulder-length hair, walked up and said "I'll help you. What do you need?"

Milo, looked at his server book, flipping through the pages. "Ummm, Coke, Water, Coke, Sprite, and two waters," Milo said.

"So, two Cokes, three waters, and Sprite," Caroline said.

"Yeah, but they all go to different tables," Milo said, ripping the page with the drink orders and their table numbers from his pad and handing it to Caroline.

"Okay," Caroline said. "Oh, and the lady with the Carnegie Salad wants you."

Milo headed to the table with the Carnegie Salad and the Reuben Sandwich.

"This salad is awful," the woman with the salad with no black olives, green peppers, capers, tomatoes, cucumbers, egg, or cheese, and oil and vinegar instead of their signature Thousand Island dressing told Milo. "It's nothing but lettuce, carrots, and mushrooms. Is everything here this bland? And where is my drink? I told you I wanted my drink to come out at the same time my food came out."

"Ummmm," Milo wasn't even sure where to start. "Do you want me to get you a new salad?" he asked, hoping to pass the problem off to Victor so he could explain to the woman why her salad was so bland. Milo figured that if Victor told her it was bland because it was just lettuce, it would sound less sarcastic.

The woman looked at her salad for a minute, as if its ingredients were going to suddenly get better by her staring at it. "No, I don't have time for that. Do you have radishes or corn?" she asked.

"We do," Milo said feeling as if he was seeing the light at the end of the tunnel.

"Just bring me some of those," and she paused. "Ya know, this is my first time here, and I had such high hopes for this place. But this food is disappointing… so disappointing."

"I'm sorry," Milo said. "I can still get you a menu if you'd like to try something else," knowing damn well that that would not make a difference because she would modify whatever else she chose to the point that it too would also have no flavor.

"No," she said. "Just bring me the radishes and corn."

"And how is your Reuben?" Milo asked turning to the man.

"It's a little bit sour, the man said. "It's good but I think the sauerkraut makes it a little sour. Maybe you should put coleslaw on it instead of sauerkraut," as if Milo was in charge of developing the menu.

"Then it wouldn't be a Reuben," the woman said to the man, with a little bit of exasperation in her voice. "Don't mind him," she continued, looking at Milo. "He likes to complain about his food wherever we go."

Milo puked a little bit inside his throat, trying to keep from laughing.

"I'll go get your drink, radishes and corn," Milo said, turning away.

As he was walking away, he heard Victor's voice. "Milo! What is this?" he asked holding a check from the kitchen in his hand. He handed the check to Milo, and Milo read it:

Grilled Cheese Sandwich RUSH

Tuna Salad Sandwich Rye Bread RUSH

"They said they were in a rush," Milo replied.

"You think that by ringing in food as a rush, it's going to magically get made faster?" Victor asked sarcastically.

"Um, well, I don't know… then why is there a rush key?" Milo asked.

With this, Victor looked a little confused. "It's for… it to use for, it's when, well… I don't know why it's there, but just don't use it again," he said, and walked away.

As he was walking toward the kitchen, he saw Dominic walking toward him with a lunch combo in his hand. "Hey uh bro, that table, I think it's 55. They said they didn't order this."

"They ordered two lunch combos," Milo said.

"Yah bro," Dominic said, "But there were three."

And suddenly Milo remembered. "Repeat item," he thought. "I hit it twice."

"What do you want me to do with it?" Dominic asked.

"Uh, just take it back to the kitchen," Milo said. Although Milo's mistake was not Dominic's fault, he was starting to dislike Dominic, and wanted to tell him he could put it where the sun don't shine.

As Milo looked up, the table that ordered the pizza and the pasta signaled him to come over.

"Hey, where's our food?" the man asked. "We ordered before they did," pointing at the table with the lunch combos. "And their food came out first."

"Ummm," Milo started, having never been asked that before. "A pizza takes longer to cook than a sandwich and a soup, but I'll go check."

"Okay," the man said, and put his hands up making the "I give up" gesture, as if it was Milo's fault that his pizza had to cook.

As he passed the table with the grilled cheese and the tuna salad sandwich, one of the women looked up at him and said "Sonny, can you please check on our order? We're in a hurry."

"Sure," Milo said pleasantly, thinking "You're 90 years old. Where the fuck do you have to get in such a hurry?"

As he headed back to the kitchen to check on food, Victor headed toward him with a grilled cheese and a tuna salad sandwich, and delivered them to the two women.

Milo made a quick U-turn and went back to the table. "How is everything, ladies?" he asked, remembering that Sandy had told him not to use the terms ladies, guys, or gals, but figuring at their age, these two probably identified as ladies.

"Marvelous, just marvelous," the lady with the tuna salad sandwich said.

As Milo got back to expo, his pizza and pasta had just come up. He grabbed it from the window, heading back to the table with it.

"Okay," he said, as he put the pasta down in front of the lady, and the pizza on the pizza rack.

"About time," the man grumbled.

"Anything else I can get you? Milo asked ignoring the comment but noting that the pizza had come out in record time for a well-done pizza.

"We're good," the lady said sympathetically, obviously aware that her husband or boyfriend or whatever he was, was just being difficult.

Milo looked up and saw the couple who had had the lunch combos were done. The man held up his hand, and made a little writing motion with his fingers, indicating they were ready for the check.

"We're ready too," the woman with the modified Carnegie Salad said.

"Was it any better after I got the radishes and corn?" Milo asked.

"A little," the lady said. "But the food here just seems kind of bland."

Not really knowing what to say, Milo went and got both checks and delivered them, the couple with lunch combos first, and then the Carnegie Salad and Reuben sandwich couple.

The man with the lunch combo held up his credit card and the check. Thinking they were ready to pay, Milo went over to the table. "There are three lunch combos on here," the man said. "We only had two. I think the kitchen made three by mistake, he added passively aggressively, knowing full well that three lunch combos had been rung in, so it was obviously Milo's fault.

"I'll go fix that and be right back," Milo said, turning away.

"Okay, just take the credit card now," the man said.

As he passed the Carnegie Salad table, he could see the woman had put two twenty-dollar bills on the table. Grabbing it, Milo said "I'll be right back with your change."

As Milo got to the server station, he split the third lunch combo off of the check, and processed the man's credit card, put it aside and looked at the other check. $32.18 and she had given Milo two twenty-dollar bills. He reached into his pocket and grabbed his cash, putting the two twenties in with it. He began to count out 82¢, but found he only had one penny. "They're not going to notice a penny, he said to himself." He looked in his pocket and he had no one-dollar bills and a bunch of fives, and a two one-hundred dollar bills. "Damn," he thought, as Sandy walked up.

"Sandy," he said. "Do you have change for a twenty?"

Sandy pulled out her cash and looked at it. Three one-hundred dollar bills, two fives, and a one-dollar bill. "Nope," she said. "All these big spenders with their hundred-dollar bills, trying to impress their dates have depleted my bank."

"Fuck," Milo thought. "This could have been so easy."

Handing the credit card and receipts to her, he asked, "Can you drop these at 61 for me?"

"Sure," she said, and as she headed to table 61, Milo headed to the bar for change.

Kim, similar in appearance to Caroline, with slightly darker hair and a few years older, who had been there almost as long as Sandy, was talking to a few regulars, or "working them for their tips," as Milo had come to realize. He stood for what seemed like an eternity, but in reality was no more than a minute. When she looked up she realized he needed change.

"You need it broken down?" she asked, taking the twenty-dollar bill from him. Milo liked Kim more than he liked Janice, the other daytime bartenders, because Kim was also a server, so she was more sympathetic to what the servers go through.

"Just a few ones, and whatever else you have," Milo said to her. "Thanks."

Taking the change from her, he put the 81¢ in coins on the service bar, and begin to count. "33" he said to himself began to count the ones. "34, 35, 36, 37, 38, 39, and 40."

He headed back to the table, and as he began to hand the woman the $7.81 she put her hand up and said "Keep it. It's for you."

"Thank you," he said politely, appreciative of the tip, but trying not to let his frustration about the exercise in futility she had just put him through show.

He turned away from the table, and almost bumped into the man with the pizza, who was now standing right behind him, holding his credit card. "Do we pay up front?" he asked.

"No Einstein," Milo thought. "You just saw me cash out two other tables, so why would it be different for you?"

Instead, he simply said "I'll get that for you," walked over to the POS, processed the man's credit card, handed it along with the slips to him, and thanked him.

As Milo cleared as much as he could from three tables that had all just left at the same time, he walked by the ladies with the tuna salad sandwich and the grilled cheese. Noticing that they were chatting and each had barely eaten a quarter of their sandwich, if that, he asked "How're we doing here ladies?"

"Great," the lady with the tuna fish sandwich said. "Just great," and Milo headed back to dish with the plates he had from the other tables.

As he finished sorting the dishes, Milo heard someone call his name from the office, so he headed in there.

"Look at this," Andy said, pointing at the computer monitor. Milo leaned over and looked at the monitor, and saw a 2-star review.


**"The Carnegie Salad was bland and disappointing. It is nothing but lettuce, carrots and oil & vinegar. But our server Nemo was very pleasant and accommodating, so I'm only giving a second star because of him."**

**Ethaline M.**

Below the review was a picture of her salad, which was little more than a bowl of lettuce.

"They literally just left here," Milo said.

"That's the world of instant gratification we live in," Andy said.

"But good job on getting us the second star, Nemo," he said as he chuckled, giving Milo a feeling of relief, that Andy was not somehow trying to blame him for her not liking her doctored salad.

As Andy prepared to reply to Ethaline M., a response from another user popped up.

**"That's not the Carnegie Salad. That's nothing but a bowl of lettuce."**
**Jessica B.**

And then another:

**"How dare you trash my beloved Carnegie Salad by showing a picture of your leftovers after you picked out all the good stuff. I love the Carnegie Salad."**

**Brenda G.**

"Well," Andy thought. "I don't need to respond and risk looking defensive. Our fans are doing it for me."

The rest of the afternoon was slow and dragged on, which was not uncommon after a busy lunch, so Milo spent his time rolling silverware, restocking, and periodically checking on the ladies with the tuna salad platter and grilled cheese sandwich, who were now his only table. At last check, they had each eaten a little bit less than half of their sandwich, and neither had touched their fries, and had been there for just over three hours chatting. It didn't bother Milo because he had to be there anyway, and by now he was the only server on the floor, so there were plenty of available tables, but the irony of two guests who were in a hurry still being there three hours later was not lost on him.

He decided to make one more pass by the table to check on the ladies. "How're we doing, ladies?" he asked. "Would either of you like some dessert?"

They looked at each other, and the lady with the tuna salad sandwich replied, "We don't have time. We're in a hurry. Can we get to-go boxes?"

"Sure," Milo said.

"Oh, and sonny," the same woman said, putting the back of her hand on her fries. "These fries are ice cold. The chef really needs to be more careful. Can you get us both some hot fries?"

*** 

Milo learned the to-go girl's name was Doris, and he thought that was kind of an odd name because Doris was an old person's name, and old as in eighty, not thirty. But he didn't care, because she was nice to him and helped him out, and she was kind of cute. But he also thought Dominic was kind of cute, as annoying as he was. Sometimes he imagined Doris getting together with Dominic but when he did, he got a little jealous because he wanted Doris. But he also wanted Dominic. But then the phone rang and his mind quickly brought him back to reality.

He was the only one at the front, so he answered the phone. The voice on the other end said "I'd like to place a to-go order."

He got the caller's name --- Courtney, and typed it in.

"Okay, Courtney, what would you like?"

"Well, what do you have?" Courtney asked.

"Um," Milo was a little taken aback by this question because he had never been asked it before and wondered why someone would call to order food when they didn't know what they wanted. "Um, well, we have sandwiches. We have salads. We have pasta. We have pizzas. We have steaks..." Milo told Courtney, hoping she would jump in and choose something.

"Ooooh, a salad sounds good," Courtney said. Milo could hear road noise in the background so he figured she was driving. "What kind of salads do you have?"

"We have ummm," Milo was pretty good at his job but he was still was new enough that he didn't know what ingredients went in all the items. He tried to reach for a menu, but the length of the phone cord was not quite long enough to allow him to reach the menus. And then he remembered back to the lady who had ordered lettuce and told him it was bland. "Um, we have the Carnegie Salad. It has black olives, green peppers, capers, tomatoes, cucumbers, egg, carrots, mushrooms, and cheese, with our Thousand Island dressing," Milo said. "Our Thousand Island dressing is different than other Thousand Island dressing because we use red pepper relish instead of pickle relish to make it." Milo was proud of his ability to be able to recite all of the ingredients, including the dressing, but it seemed to be lost on Courtney.

"Noooo," Courtney said. "It sounds good, but it's not really what I want. What other salads do you have?"

"Um, well," Milo said, as he pulled out his phone to google the menu. "We have the Crispy Chicken Salad. It is crispy chicken, cheddar cheese, provolone cheese, mozzarella cheese, cherry tomatoes, and carrots on a bed of greens, served with our warm mustardy bacon dressing," Milo said, realizing Courtney could probably tell he was reading off the menu.

"Crispy?" Courtney asked. "You mean it's fried?"

"Um, yeah, I think so," Milo said, not quite sure how the chicken was cooked because it was cut up.

"Nooo," she said, "sounds good, but maybe I'm just not in the mood for a salad right now. What kind of pizza, do you have?"

"What kind of pizza?" Milo thought to himself, not quite knowing how to answer.

A party of four walked in and looked at Milo, and he whispered "Someone will be right with you." The guests could see he was on the phone, so they smiled and waited patiently. Milo desperately wanted to stop what he was doing to seat them because he was next on rotation, but he couldn't. He looked up and saw Carmine, who was average height and had a bob-cut that she probably thought looked cute, but Milo thought looked silly, walk by and gestured to her to seat them.

"Hi. How many? Carmine asked the party.

"Four," the woman said.

"Right this way," Carmine said, grabbing four menus, leading the party over to one of her own tables. As he watched and looked around the restaurant, Milo noticed that table 53's drinks were almost empty. Wanting to get them refills, because Sandy had taught him to anticipate the guest's needs, Milo knew he had to finish up with Courtney on the phone.

"Well," he said to Courtney, "we have thin and crispy and deep dish pizza," thinking he had nailed it.

"Yeah, but I mean what toppings do you have for your…. ooohhh," Courtney said, cutting herself off mid-sentence, realizing that Milo's answer triggered something in her brain. "Do you have the stuffed crust, like Domino's?"

Milo wasn't quite sure what stuffed crust pizza from Domino's was, but he knew they didn't have it. "No," he said. "Just the thin and crispy and the deep dish pizza," wondering why Courtney didn't just order from Domino's if that was what she wanted.

"I think I'll have the small thin and crispy pizza," Courtney said. "What can I put on it?" she asked, rephrasing her previous question. As Milo began to read the toppings to her, Carmine walked by.

"Milo," she said. "Table 53 wants refills on their drinks," and kept on walking.

"Well, we have Pepperoni, Sausage, Mushrooms, Extra cheese, Onion, Black olives, Green pepper, Fresh garlic, Tomato, Fresh basil," Milo said as he read from the menu on his phone, pausing to catch his breath, hoping Courtney would stop him and pick something. But she didn't.

"Artichokes, ground beef, pickles, pineapple, fresh mozzarella, eggplant…"

"Eggplant?" Courtney interrupted. "People actually put eggplant on a pizza?" she asked?

"Um, yeah, they do," Milo answered, although he had never had anyone order eggplant on a pizza, not realizing they actually offered pickles on their pizzas, and thinking that pickles were a stranger pizza topping than eggplant, and hoping he had found something Courtney would like.

"Ya know what," Courtney said. "Just give me a small thin and crispy pepperoni pizza. I've been craving pepperoni pizza all day."

*＊＊

"Milo, you're cut," Andy said. "Finish your tables, roll your silverware, and check with Sabrina on what side work she wants you to do before you do your checkout." As Andy finished his sentence, Sabrina, tall with dark, wavy hair, and slightly heavier than most of the other female servers at Bubba's walked up, so Andy turned toward her. "Milo's cut. It's just you and Janice for the last hour, so Milo's going to roll silverware and do his side work."

"Sure thing," Sabrina said.

"I don't have any tables," Milo said not really directing his sentence to either one of them in particular. "I've already got a lot of silverware rolled and made ramekins of ketchups and dressings for tomorrow." Milo said, turning to Sabrina. "What else do you need me to do?"

"Nothing," Sabrina said. "I'll finish the rest before I leave."

***

Milo loved being the first one to walk into an empty restaurant first thing in the morning. It felt like overnight everything was magically cleaned and brand new, kind of the way it felt the morning after a huge rainstorm.

"Good Morning," he said to Victor as he walked into the kitchen to clock in. "Can I borrow your card to clock in?"

"Why are you late?" Victor asked, handing his card to Milo so he could clock in. "And Good Morning."

"I'm not," Milo said. "I'm early."

"When are you scheduled?" Victor asked.

"In nine more minutes," Milo said.

"You can clock in five minutes before you're scheduled without a card," Victor said, reaching out to Milo for his card back. "Wait four more minutes. Labor's through the roof this week."

Milo began to walk through the restaurant to get what he needed. He pulled out the tray with ramekins of ketchup and dressings that he had made the previous evening, and there were no ketchups left, three ramekins of Thousand Island dressing, and four ramekins of ranch.

"That's odd," he thought. "I made a whole tray of each of these last night just an hour before closing."

Milo came back from the walk-in with a one-gallon jug of Thousand Island dressing in one hand and a one-gallon jug of ranch in the other and put them down on the counter. He grabbed a jug of ketchup off of the shelf and set it on the counter. He placed the ramekins neatly on three trays and inserted the pump in the ranch.

As soon as he got the pump in the jug of ranch he heard voices at the front of the restaurant.

"Hi," Milo said, walking up to the front of the restaurant, a little surprised to see guests in the restaurant this early.

"Party of four," the woman said. The guests appeared to be a mom and a dad and two daughters who Milo guestimated to be about six and eight years old although he wasn't sure and really didn't care.

"Um," Milo said, looking down at his watch, "We don't open for another, uh, twenty-two minutes. We're still setting up. But I can get you seated and give you some menus to look at while you wait."

"Hmmm, well I guess so," the woman said, looking at her husband. "Do you want to wait?"

"Yeah," he said. "The clerk at the hotel recommended this place and finding somewhere else will take just as long, and we really need to get on the road."

"Follow me," Milo said, leading them to table 40 since it was the closest table to the door, hoping to leave them with their menus and greet them and get their drinks once the restaurant opened, so he could go finish setting up.

"Can we get some drinks while we wait?" the father asked.

"Uh, yeah, sure," Milo said apprehensively, knowing that he had already burned up precious minutes of the limited time he had to get the restaurant set up getting the early arrivals seated, and would now burn up more of those precious minutes getting them drinks. "We have Coke, Diet Coke, Sprite, Fanta Orange, Dr. Pepper, and Lemonade," He continued.

"I'll have a water with lemon," the mom said.

"So will I," the dad said. "Girls, what would you like to drink?" the dad asked turning to his daughters.

"Do you have grape soda?" one of the girls asked Milo.

"He just told you what they have," the mom said.

"I'll have a Shirley Temple," The girl said, "with three cherries," she added quickly.

"Can you make a Shirley Temple?" the mom asked.

"We can," Milo said, knowing he hated making the first Shirley Temple of the day as much as the first waters with lemon because he had to find where last night's closer had put the grenadine, cherries, and lemons, if there were even lemons cut up.

"And Becky," the mom said, turning to the other girl, "What would you like?"

"Chocolate milk," the girl said.

"Okay," Milo said, knowing that chocolate milk was probably the only drink he hated making more than a Shirley Temple. "I'll be right back with those."

As Milo turned to leave the table to get the drinks, the phone rang. He looked around to see if he could see Victor, or if the second server had arrived yet and could possibly answer the phone or help him set up. The phone kept ringing, and Milo did not see anyone else, so he turned to the host/hostess station to answer the phone.

"Hi, I'd like to make a reservation for twelve people tonight," the voice on the other end of the phone said.
"Fuck," Milo thought to himself. "I shouldn't have even answered the phone. We're not even open yet."

"Um, we don't take reservations," Milo let the caller know.

"Not even for a large party?" the caller asked.

"Uh no, we don't take reservations at all," Milo said.

"But we're a party of twelve," the caller said, as if she was the first person to ever come into the restaurant with a party of twelve. "This is A LOT of business for the restaurant, you know" she said, emphasizing and drawing out the words "A LOT," as she said them.

Although he had only been at the restaurant for a few months, Milo knew that a party of twelve was no more business for the restaurant and the server, than three parties of four, and that they would probably sit a lot longer, make more of a mess, and take up a lot of time with separate checks.

"No," I'm sorry he said. "We just don't take reservations at all."

"It's my daughter's 16th birthday," the lady said, changing her tone of voice to try to sway Milo to make an exception. "It's really special to her."

"No, we don't take any reservations at all, but I can get the manager for you if you would like," Milo said, hoping to pass the caller who was beginning to annoy him off to Victor, knowing that he needed to get drinks for his table and finish setting up.

"No, that's okay," the caller said indignantly. "I don't have time to wait for a manager. "How long is the wait going to be at 6:30 tonight?"

"Um," Milo said, dumbfounded and realizing the absurdity of the question, and not knowing how to even begin to answer, he just said "I don't know," without even an explanation, but added "You can add your name to the waitlist on the Google App."

"Well can you put us on the waitlist now for 6:30 and have a table set up for us when we get there?" the caller asked, as if changing the way she asked for a reservation would change Milo's answer.

"We don't have a waitlist yet. I can't put you on the waitlist until we have a waitlist," Milo said, realizing that what the woman was asking for was a reservation, just phrasing her question differently.

"Okay. Well I guess we'll take our chances," the woman said and abruptly hung up.

Turning away from the host/hostess station, and walking past his table who had heard the whole conversation, Milo said "I'll be right back with your drinks."

"This pastrami sandwich," the man called to Milo from a few feet away before Milo could make his escape, "How highly-seasoned is the pastrami?"

"You just heard me answering dumb questions and now you're going to ask me a dumb question too," Milo thought to himself. "It's Pastrami. It's seasoned!"

Milo turned and went back to the table. "Well," he said, "It's pretty well seasoned, but we have corned beef too, and that is less seasoned."

"Okay, I'll take that" the man said. "With Swiss cheese, and sauerkraut on rye bread and Thousand Island dressing."

"That's our Reuben Sandwich," Milo said pleasantly, pointing to the menu, not wanting to engage yet, and wishing he could use his sarcastic voice.

"What does that come with?" the man asked.

Pointing back to the same place on the menu, Milo said "Fries. But you can get potato salad or coleslaw instead it you would like."

"Fries are good," the man said. "With a side of ranch."

Looking down at his watch, Milo realized it was now 11 o'clock and the restaurant was now open and he hadn't even began to set up. "It's opening time," Milo told his guests, "so I can get your order now."

"Becky, what would you like?" the mom asked the older of the two girls.

"I want a side of ranch with mine too," the girl said.

"Honey, you have to tell the man what you want to order first," the mom said.

"I'll have the, the," and looking at her mom said "I don't know what it's called" she said." The mom cupped her hand over the girl's ear, said something, and the girl said "I'll have the kid's pepperoni pizza. But I want it without pepperoni. And a side of ranch."

"I'll have the Carnegie Salad," the mom said to Milo, and turning to the other girl said "Hannah, tell the man what you'd like."

"I don't know," Hannah said almost in a whisper, looking down.

"You do know," the mom said. "You just told me." The girl sort of curled up in her chair and looked away. "Hannah, you need to order your food. You're almost five years old."

"Kid's fish sticks," Hannah said in a whisper.

"We don't have fish sticks," Milo replied "How about chicken toes?"

"Toes?" the mom asked.

"It's just our name for chicken fingers," Milo told her, trying not to let his frustration show.

"She'll take those," the mom said, finally deciding that she needed to be the one to order for her child instead of making the five year old order for herself. "Oh, and do you have coloring books or something? We've been here for almost half an hour and the kids are starting to get restless."

As Milo headed back to the kitchen he came face to face with a smart phone. Backing up a little bit, he saw a hand, and then an arm attached to the smart phone, and backing up a little more, he saw a Door Dash driver attached to the arm.

"Milo, I just seated table 65," Doris said.

"You're the hostess today?" Milo asked.

"No, still to-go," but no one showed up yet. Victor is checking to see who is supposed to be here."

"Why'd you seat them at the back of the restaurant?" Milo asked.

"They asked to sit back there," Doris replied.

"Okay," Milo said, and turning to the Door Dash Driver, he said in his dad voice "she can help you," pointing to Doris.

As Milo headed back into the kitchen, looking for a familiar face, he found a face, but it was not familiar. "Hi, I'm Milo," he said to the slightly stocky guy who he judged to be about his age, wearing a Bubba's shirt.

"Josh," the slightly stocky guy said putting his hand out for a fist bump.

"You new here?" Milo asked.

"Yeah," Josh said. "Sandy started my training yesterday. I'm supposed to be with Carmine today."

"Do you know where Carmine is?" Milo asked, assuming she was the second server in.

"No, Victor went to call her," Josh replied "He said to see what I could help with in the meantime. And he's calling the hostess too. She's not here yet either."

"Um, okay," Milo said, already feeling the shift going sideways, and they had only been open for a few minutes. "I'm getting drinks for table 40, and table 65 just got seated. "Can you go get a drink order from table 65? It's near the back corner of the restaurant."

"Sure thing," Josh said.

Milo squatted to look in the reach-in for the grenadine, cherries, lemons, chocolate syrup and milk. "Well, four out of five isn't bad," he mumbled to himself, grabbing everything except the grenadine, figuring he could use the syrup from the cherries for the Shirley Temple and dumbfounded but grateful that someone actually took the time to wrap up five lemon wedges.

He quickly put in table 40's order, finished preparing the drinks, grabbed two coloring books and some crayons, and headed out of the kitchen when Josh walked back in.

"They want a Mountain Dew and Starry," Josh said. "Want me to get them?"

"We have Coke products," Milo said "Bring them two Sprites and see if that is okay. If not, find out what they want instead."

As Milo came back into the dining room with table 40's drinks, he noticed two older ladies at table 50. Dropping off table 40's drinks and the coloring books and crayons, he headed to table 50, realizing he also needed to get to table 65.

"Hi. My name is Milo and I'll be taking care of you today. Can I start either of you with a Long Island Iced Tea, or Bloody Mary while you look over the menu? Or perhaps a Raspberry Limeade?"

"Tell us about today's lunch specials," one of the ladies said to Milo.

"Um, we don't have any lunch specials," Milo replied. "We have a lunch combo with soup or salad."

"No, that wasn't it. We were just here last week and we both had half an egg salad sandwich and some fries," the other lady said.

"No, no you didn't," Milo thought to himself. "We don't have egg salad. We haven't had egg salad as long as I have been here."

"You know, Stella," the other lady said to her friend. "I think the young man may be right. I think we split the egg salad sandwich and both had half."

"You're right Beatrice," the woman said. "We split the egg salad sandwich." Turning to Milo she said, "We'll have the egg salad sandwich and an extra plate."

"Well we don't have egg salad." Milo said. "Perhaps it was the tuna salad sandwich you had?"

"They're out of egg salad today, Beatrice," Stella said to her friend, not even completely hearing what Milo had told her. "What do you want to do?"

"Well I don't know," Beatrice said slowly, looking at the menu.

"How about if I start you with some drinks?" Milo asked, realizing he still had to finish setting up and had other tables to take care of.

"Great idea," Stella said. "I'll have a hot tea."

"Make that two," Beatrice said.

"Hot tea, the only thing I hate more than Shirley Temples and Chocolate Milk," Milo thought to himself. He wasn't sure if it was the treasure hunt for all the items he needed for a hot tea --- the teabags, the small plate, the mug, the miniature tea urn, the beverage napkin, the spoon, the lemon, and the fact that none of them were in the same part of the restaurant, or the fact that because of the setup on the small plate, you couldn't carry two in one hand, but he knew he hated hot tea.

"Elizabeth is scheduled to be the hostess today," Victor said to Milo as he walked up to the soda station as Milo was preparing two hot teas, but she had car trouble. Help Doris watch the door until Elizabeth gets here. And I can't get hold of Carmine. She was supposed to be the second server in at 11:00, so it's just you and Janice until Sabrina gets in at 11:45, so keep an eye on Josh."

"Sabrina?" Milo asked? "She never works the day shift."

"Apparently she picked it up for Emily but didn't get it approved in the app," Victor said. "But she should be here at 11:45. And what's up in the kitchen?" Victor asked. "There's no iced tea made, no lemons cut, the to-go boxes are not stocked, there's only half a bin of silverware, and the ketchup and dressings are still sitting out on the counter. There's barely any ice in either of the bins, and most of the clean soda cups are still at dish. I thought Andy brought the opening server in half an hour early so you could get all that stuff done before we opened."

"I uh," Milo started, figuring it would take too much time to explain that he had done what Sabrina asked him to do when he left last night, and that she said she'd do the rest, and about the way the morning started. "Can you take these two hot teas to the ladies at table 50 please?" He asked Victor, handing him the hot teas.

"There's a lady on the phone," Doris said walking up to Victor, who was now holding the hot teas, "Who said she called and was told she could make a reservation on the Google app, but it's not letting her do it. She's calling back because she was told a manager could make a reservation for her."

"You told her I could make a reservation for her?" Victor asked, still holding the hot teas and now looking at Milo. "We don't take reservations. Period."

"I did not," Milo started out indignantly, "tell her you could make a reservation for her," toning his voice down for the second half of his sentence. "When she told me she wanted to make a reservation because of how much business a party of twelve is for the restaurant, I offered to let her speak to a manager, but she told me she didn't have time and hung up on me."

"Take these hot teas to table 50, Doris," Victor said, handing her the hot teas and heading in the direction of the phone.

"Table 65 is ready to order and wants to know how much longer on their appetizer," Josh said as he approached Milo at the beverage station.

"What appetizer?" Milo asked Josh.

"The spinach and artichoke dip," Josh said. "They asked me for it when I got their drinks for you. I thought you knew."

"How would I know?" Milo asked, ringing in the spinach and artichoke dip as he talked to Josh. His first impression of Josh was a pretty bright guy, but now he was not quite so sure.

"I'll go ask Anthony to put a rush on the spin dip," Janice said, coming out from behind the bar.

"Thanks," Milo said, grateful but a little surprised that Janice offered to help him without being asked.

"My name is Milo and I'll be taking care of you today," Milo said as he got to table 65 with Josh, noticing that it was two men, about ten or so years older than he was, having some sort of a conference or meeting, because they had papers and their cell phones spread out on the table. "I'll have that spinach and artichoke dip out as soon as it's ready. And you've already met Josh, who's training today. Were you ready to order?"

As soon as he finished his question, he saw the two men look past him, and, wondering why, he looked back and saw Victor approaching the table with the spinach and artichoke dip. As he and Josh moved aside, Victor tried to put the spinach and artichoke down, to no avail because there were papers and cell phones all over the table. As the men looked at him, waiting for him to put the spinach and artichoke dip down, he looked unsuccessfully for an empty place on the table to put it down. Although it was only a few seconds, time moved in slow motion and it felt like ten minutes to Milo.

"Ummmm, would you mind moving some of those papers over so I can set this down?" Victor asked.

"Oh," one of the men said in a surprised tone of voice, as they both started to move the papers to the far side of the table, as if it had never occurred to them that they would need room on the table for the food.

"Now you know what it feels like to be me," Milo thought, as Victor walked away.

"Were you ready to order?" Milo asked.

"I think we're both going to have a burger with fries, medium, one man said looking at the other, who nodded in agreement.

As Milo and Josh headed back toward the front of the restaurant, Milo noticed that Doris and Victor were delivering his food to the family at table 40, and that table 25 had just been sat. Passing the bar, he looked up at Janice "Do you want table 25?" he asked her.

"No hun, you take it. It's kind of far from the bar," she said. "My regulars will start coming in soon."

"Thanks," he said, also wondering why Doris was seating tables in every corner of the restaurant, and kept walking to table 40, suddenly realizing he had forgotten to get the order from the two hot tea drinkers at table 50. Glancing at table 50, the women looked perfectly content, and he noticed there were no menus in sight. Realizing he had some time, Milo stopped by table 40 first.

"How is everything?" He asked.

"My fish sticks taste funny," Hannah said innocently.

"They're magic fish sticks," her mother said quickly, Milo realizing that the mother had not told Hannah that she was eating chicken. "Everything is fine," the mother said, looking up at Milo.

"Can I get another side of ranch?" the father asked.

"Can you get the ranch for table 40 and refill the ice, and try to restock the cups?" Milo said to Josh, as they backed away from the table.

"Sure," Josh said as he headed to the kitchen and Milo headed to table 50.

"Ladies, are we ready to order?" Milo asked.

"That sweet girl over there," one of the women said as she pointed to Doris, "got our order already."

"Great," Milo said, knowing that Doris was one of the few people who would help him. "I'll be back with your food a soon as I can," he continued, wondering what they had ordered.

"Hi. My name is Milo and I'll be taking care of you today," Milo said as he got to table 25. "Can I start you with…"

"I'll take this," one of the women said before Milo could finish his greeting, pointing to the Fiery Prawns and Pasta.

"And I'll have the burger well done," the other woman said, "no onion or lettuce, with the potato salad instead of fries."

"And we'll both have waters," the first woman said.

"Okay," Milo said. "One Fiery Prawns and Pasta, and one burger well done, no onion or lettuce, and potato salad. And the Fiery Prawns and Pasta is spicy," Milo added.

"It's fine," the lady said. "I had it last week and it was not spicy at all."

Heading back from table 25 toward the front of the restaurant, Milo saw Victor walking out of the kitchen with two to-go bags, one in each hand. But instead of stopping at the to-go area, he headed straight to table 50. As he got closer, Milo saw Victor deliver the to-go bags to table 50 and say "Okay ladies," Victor said. "Your order is ready. Two lunch combos. Here you go," and set the bags on the table.

"Why are these in to-go containers," Stella asked, looking surprised and taken aback, and frankly a little annoyed.

As Victor started to answer, Milo got to the table, realizing that since Doris had rung the orders in, she probably used the to-go screen, not even knowing that there was an option to ring in food for dine-in.

"I am SO sorry ladies," Milo said, as he approached the table. "The girl who rung in your food is our to-go person, so I think that is why it came out in to-go boxes. I'll take that back to the kitchen and have them put it on plates for you."

"Um, no, that's okay," Stella said, kind of hesitating as she spoke. "I think we can eat the food from the to-go boxes since it's already here. Can't we Beatrice?"

"Sure," Beatrice said. It will taste just the same, and will save us having to wrap up any extras."

"I think we're fine like this," Stella said. "For a moment I thought you were trying to rush us out of here," she added with a slight laugh.

Ringing in table 25's order at 12:02, Milo saw Sabrina walking briskly into the restaurant for her 11:45 shift in street clothes, her hair a mess, and a backpack over one shoulder, and head straight back to the kitchen.

Milo made his way to the kitchen to check on table 65's burgers, although if he had to be honest with himself, the real reason was to see what was going on with Sabrina. As he got into the kitchen, Sabrina came out of dry goods wearing wrinkled jeans, a wrinkled and slightly dirty Bubba's shirt, her backpack still over one shoulder, open with her street clothes sticking out of the top, hopping as she put on one of her non-slip shoes and then the other. She reached in her backpack, grabbed a hair brush, set her bag down next to the walk-in freezer and made beeline to one of the restrooms.

"Milo, you're up," Ray called from behind the line. Milo grabbed his two burgers for table 65, put a ramekin of ketchup for the fries on each plate, and made his way back out to table 65 to deliver the burgers.

"Okay guys," Milo said as he got to the table. "I have your burgers here." Standing in front of the table, Milo looked for a place to put the burgers, but both guys just stared back at him, waiting for him to put the burgers down, without making any effort to move any of their papers, phones, or the spinach and artichoke dip.

"Uh, can you please move some of the papers over so I can set your burgers down?" Milo asked as he was standing there holding the burgers. Both guys looked at him a little surprised that he actually needed a place on the table to put their food, but made a half-assed effort to slide some of their papers over, so Milo took one burger and put in on the very left corner of the table closest to him and the other burger and put it on the very right corner of the table closest to him, pushing them both just a little bit into the pile of papers as he set them down so they would not fall off the edge of the table.

"Anything else I can get you"? Milo asked.

"Can I get a side of ranch?" one of the guys asked.

"I'll take one too," the other guy said.

"Sure," Milo said, slightly annoyed that they hadn't asked for the ranch when they ordered. "Is there anything else I can get either of you?"

Both nodded no, and Milo headed back to the kitchen to get two sides of ranch.

"Why is nothing set up?" Sabrina asked Milo as he entered the kitchen. "There's no iced tea, no lemons, no ice, no ramekins of ketchups or dressings, and all the clean cups are still at dish."

"You said you would finish up after I left last night," Milo said, slightly annoyed. "And the trays of ramekins of ketchup and dressings were all full when I left."

"We had a party of 8 come in 20 minutes before closing," Sabrina said. "They kept asking for more ranch and ketchup, and I was lucky to get them out of here ten minutes after closing, and the only reason I got them out of here that quickly was because we 'ran out' of desserts," Sabrina said, making air quotes with her fingers as she said the words 'ran out.' "Andy said to leave it for the morning because you guys would have time to finish up in the morning."

"Well I only have a half hour to get everything set up before we open, and that's barely enough time on a good day, but Carmine didn't show up, table 40 showed up twenty minutes before we opened and wanted to play twenty questions and said they were in a hurry, yet they are still here, and lady called about a reservation and wanted to debate with me after I told her we don't take reservations," Milo said, pumping two ramekins of ranch for table 65 and putting them on a small plate.

"Okay, anything else I can get either of you?" Milo asked as he dropped of the ranches at table 65.

"Do you have any Tabasco?" one of the guys asked Milo?

"We don't," Milo said. "But we have Cholula," he added, wondering why the guy couldn't have asked for Tabasco or Cholula or whatever else he wanted when he asked for ranch.

"That'll work," the guy said.

***

"We're ready for the check," the husband at table 40 said, as Milo passed by on his way back to the kitchen. "We need to get on the road to get back home."

"Be right back with it," Milo said, as he went to check on table 25's food.

"Milo, you're up," Ray said as Milo came into the kitchen. Ray was the only cook who called out when server's food was ready, and put all the items from one order next to each other. Although Milo found it kind of annoying, he also appreciated it.

"Okay ladies, I've got the Fiery Prawns and Pasta," Milo said as he put the Fiery Prawns and Pasta down, "And the burger with no lettuce and no tomato."

"That's not what it looked like last week," the lady said, looking at her dish. "Last week the Prawns were around the edge of the plate and the pasta had more of an orange color. These Prawns go right across the top of the pasta, and the pasta is kind of reddish. It looks kind of spicy. I don't like spicy," as she twirled the fettucine around her fork.

"The one with the orange color and the Prawns around the edge of the plate is the Sweet and Sour Prawns and Pasta," Milo said. "You ordered the Fiery Prawns and Pasta."

"Well that's not what I wanted. Why didn't you tell me it wasn't the Sweet and Sour Prawns and Pasta?" the lady asked Milo.

Milo bit his tongue and simply said, "Would you like me to get you the Sweet and Sour Prawns and Pasta instead?"

"No, no I'll try it," she said, putting the pasta she had just twirled into her mouth, and immediately gasping dramatically, fanning the outside of her mouth in a way that Milo perceived to be fake and performative, and spitting the pasta back onto the plate. "I think you had better get me the Sweet and Sour Prawns and Pasta that I ordered."

As Milo headed back to the kitchen with the Fiery Prawns and Pasta, Doris walked by him with a party of 6 --- a group with what appeared to be two moms and four rowdy kids, and headed back to table 26. "This is Sabrina's, since she just got here," Doris said as she passed Milo.

When Milo came back out to table 25 to tell the lady that her Sweet and Sour Prawns and Pasta would be right up, Doris was pushing tables 46 and 47 together in the cell as the moms patiently waited, and the kids ran around the area between table 26 and the front of the cell, laughing and playing.

"I'm glad they asked to sit in there and not next to us," the lady said before Milo could say anything. "Do you think you could close the door to the cell, lock it, and throw the key away?"

As much as Milo didn't like this lady, she seemed to have softened a little bit, and Milo couldn't help but chuckle. "That would be nice," Milo whispered, although he knew he really shouldn't be saying something like that. "Your food is going to be ready in just a few minutes."

Milo turned and saw Sabrina greeting her table, the kids still up and down, sitting at the chairs one minute and running around inside the cell and in the area in front of the cell the next minute, the two moms oblivious to the kids as they ordered.

As Milo turned to go back toward table 40 to drop the check, Victor approached table 25 with the Sweet and Sour Prawns and Pasta. As he got to table 40, the wife handed him a credit card and he went to the POS at the bar to process it. As he turned from the POS with the processed card, Sabrina approached to get the drinks for her table in the cell. "Friggin' little tykes," she mumbled to Milo "won't even sit still while I'm trying to get their drink order, and the moms do nothing about it. I think they think it's cute."

"How're we doing ladies?" Milo asked as he got to table 50 after dropping the credit card slip off at table 40.

"Everything's great," Beatrice said. "The to-go boxes are a great idea!"

As Milo was heading back to check on table 25, he was just a few steps ahead of Sabrina, who was carrying the drinks and coloring books for her table in the cell.

"This is much better," the lady at table 25 said of her Sweet and Sour Prawns and Pasta before Milo could even ask.

"Great," Milo said, and headed back toward table 65. As he passed the cell, he noticed Sabrina entering the cell with two iced teas, four kid waters and four kid chocolate milks, but only the two moms at the table… no kids in sight.

As Sabrina got just inside the cell with the tray of drinks, Milo heard a kid's voice yell "bang," and a kid darted out from under table 35, through the bars of the cell toward table 36. Simultaneously another kid came out from under table 36, and yelled "bang." Startled, Sabrina looked to see what was going on, but as she looked at the two kids to her left, the two remaining kids came running into the cell, one of them to her right, and one of them to her left, and began to run around her, and one of them grabbed the corner of her apron, jostling her enough that the tray started to shift, and as one glass of iced tea fell over on the tray, it caused the balance of the other drinks to shift and all of the drinks started to wobble, and then started to fall like dominoes, spilling iced tea, water and chocolate milk on the table, and on one of the women and a splashing a little bit of liquid on a few of the kids, who took off out of the cell, eventually taking the tray down with it.

"What the fu…" the woman started, standing up, but caught herself. "Don't you know how to carry a tray of drinks?" she fumed.

Startled, Sabrina just stood there, not even knowing what to say, so Milo turned, and ran toward the bar, grabbed as many dry bar towels as he could find, and ran back toward the cell.

Still stunned, Sabrina said "I'm so sorry… I'm so sorry," to the woman, trying to grab the few dry napkins that were left on the table to hand them to the woman.

"Don't they teach you to carry trays in waitress school?" the woman yelled out condescendingly at Sabrina, who was now on the verge of tears. "I'm soaked … we come her for a nice meal, and…" she put her entire hand out to point to the mess, "now this."

As much distain as Milo had for Sabrina, he really felt sorry for her, and put his hand on her shoulder, and said "Here, let me get this," as he moved into the cell handing the woman a few bar towels, as Sabrina backed out.

As Milo began to wipe the table, Victor approached Sabrina, who was now just outside of the cell almost in tears, and said "go sit down and take a breather hun."

"I'm so sorry ladies, I'm so sorry... let me get this cleaned up for you, Victor said."

"That waitress," the lady belted at Victor, "doesn't know how to carry a tray of drinks. A simple task like that..."

"Ma'am, let me help you dry off," Victor said, handing her more towels, "and I'll address it with her later."

As Milo finished wiping the table and chairs, Ray came into the cell with a mop bucket and a mop. As he entered, the woman backed up a little bit. "Hi ma'am," Ray said, "I'll get this floor cleaned up."

As Ray was mopping the floor, Christina came from the bar with a new tray of drinks and coloring books, set them on table 35, and helped Milo and Victor put the tables back together.

"I want him," the woman said to Victor while pointing to Milo, "to wait on us. I don't want that clumsy waitress."

"Of course," Victor said. "Do you and the kids like cold cuts and French fries?"

Thinking for a minute, and looking at her friend, the woman said "Yes, we do," softening her tone of voice.

"How about if I make you all a special platter with a variety of cold cut sandwiches and fries, on me, for your inconvenience?" Victor asked.

Again, looking at her friend who nodded in agreement, the woman, who had now calmed down, said "Yes, that would be fine. Thank you."


The review was not good.

**Worst Service Ever! While my friend and I and our children sat and waited patiently for our drinks, the clumsy waitress tripped as she walked up to our table, spilling a tray of drinks all over the table and me.**

**Willow Hildebrand**

"What a shift," Doris said to Milo as they were getting ready to leave.

"Yeah, I've never had one quite like it Milo said. "It kinda made me hungry and I'm never hungry when I leave here."

"Wanna get something to eat?" Doris asked.

"Uh, sure," Milo said, a little surprised. He had never hung out with anyone from Bubba's before. "Where"?

"You like Dinner Diner?" Doris asked.

"Dinner Diner? I've never heard of it," Milo said.

"Really? Doris replied. "I thought everyone had been there. My parents began taking me there when I was a kid. It's a diner but they don't open until 4 PM. But they serve everything a diner has… steak and eggs, chicken and waffles, biscuits and gravy… ya know, diner food."

"Sure," Milo said. "Sounds good."

***

"Two for dinner?" The woman Milo figured to be about their age, dressed in a blue-green dress with grey sewn-on suspenders and grey sleeves, and a grey apron asked.

"Yes," Doris said.

"Come with me," the woman said.

"I'm going to use the restroom," Doris said. "I'll come find you."

"Sure thing," Milo said, as he followed the woman to a table.

"Here ya go," she said as she put two menus on the table. "I'll come back when your friend gets back."

"Thanks," Milo said as he slid into the booth.

"Wow," He thought to himself as he flipped through the menu. "This menu is really long, thinking of Bubba's menu, which was two pages double-sided. He counted 8 pages, and the print was not small, although there were pictures of some of the items on the menu. Looking around, he couldn't help but compare the Dinner Diner to Bubba's. It was the first time Milo had been to a restaurant since he started working at Bubba's. They have Pepsi products. Bubba's has Coke products. They have four different kinds of iced tea. Bubba's just has black tea and guava iced tea. They carry their food out on trays. At Bubba's they carry their food without trays. At Bubba's they wear t-shirts. Here the women were all wearing a dress and the men wore a shirt the same blue-green color that looked to Milo like a bowling shirt.  He looked back at the menu, trying to decide even where to begin to look.

"Hi. My name is Doris and I'll be taking care of you tonight." Milo looked up, smiled, saw Doris and they both laughed.

Expecting Doris to sit on the other side of the booth, Milo was sitting in the middle of the seat, but as she bent over to sit down, Doris sat on the same side of the booth Milo was on. A little surprised, Milo slid in further to make room for Doris next to him.

"Wow," Milo said, trying not to act surprised that Doris sat on the same side of the booth as he was on, "This place has a huge menu."

"I usually get the chicken-fried steak," Doris said. "It's my favorite. But they have great burgers too, and their breakfast items are awesome if you're down for breakfast for dinner."

"Chicken… fried… steak?" Milo asked slowly and inquisitively. "Is it white meat or dark meat?"

"No silly," Doris said with a slight laugh, and a playful slap on the shoulder." It's chicken --- fried steak. It's steak that's fried like chicken."

"Oh," Milo said, not sure how else to respond, but coming to the sudden realization that maybe some of the questions his guests asked that had answers that were obvious to him were not so silly after all, "but yeah, their questions are silly," he quickly thought. "Chicken Fried Steak is a dish he had never heard of. How do you respond when someone asks you how big a third pound burger is or how big a 16 inch pizza is or why you don't have chicken pot pie on your menu?"

"Hi. How are you tonight?" the same server who had seated them asked, and without giving them a chance to reply, continued, "Can I start you with a milkshake or a beer or a soda while you look over the menu?"

"Milkshakes!" Milo thought. "That was another difference. The Dinner Diner has milkshakes and Bubba's doesn't."

"I'll have a Pepsi and the Chicken Fried Steak," Doris replied, surprising Milo because he had not really looked at the menu.

The server looked up at Milo, and unprepared to answer, he just said "I'll have the burger, medium, with fries and a Mountain Dew," immediately disappointed in his choice because a burger was something he could get at Bubba's, but not wanting to be 'that guest,' the one who keeps changing his order, Milo stuck with his first choice. At least the Mountain Dew was something he couldn't get at Bubba's.

"My name is Jessica," the server said. "I'll go put your order in and I'll be back with your drinks."

"She got our order first, and then told us her name," Milo thought to himself. "Interesting, because I always tell them my name immediately and then ask what they would like to drink. Maybe I should try that," but immediately decided it was a bad idea because he liked telling people his name first.

"What a day," Milo said turning to Doris, trying not to let there be any awkward silence, although Doris was one of the few people at work he was comfortable with.

"I know!" Doris said, sounding almost a little bit excited. "When that woman started yelling at Sabrina, I wanted to crawl into a hole. I've seen some nasty people but she takes the cake."

"I know," Milo said. "Sabrina is not one of my favorite people but I really began to feel bad for her when that happened. And it was her kids who tripped Sabrina and caused her to drop the tray."

"It was?" Doris asked a little surprised and lightly slapping Milo's left knee with her right hand, and leaving her hand on his knee. "I thought Sabrina just lost her balance."

"No!" Milo said, surprised that her hand was now on his knee, but without missing a beat. "I was standing right there. Her kids were running around the cell and one of them pulled on Sabrina's apron while she was running and Sabrina still had the tray of drinks."

"Okay," Jessica said, returning with the drinks. "Here's a Pepsi," putting the Pepsi down in front of Doris, "and a Mountain Dew," putting the Mountain Dew in front of Milo. "So you two work at Bubba's?" Jessica asked pointing to their shirts. "How is it over there?"

"Pretty good," Milo said. "It's the only restaurant I've ever worked at, but I like it," and trying to reciprocate the question, he added, "How is it over here?"

"It's good," Jessica said, "We've got a pretty big menu and it takes a long time to learn, but I like it here."

"Our menu is pretty small," Milo said. "It made it really easy to learn, but people are always asking for something we don't even have without even looking at the menu."

"Our menu is so long and complicated," it takes people forever to read it, and then they have so many S.I.s," their food comes out flavorless and they complain about it."

"S.I.s?" Milo asked, never having heard the term before.

"Special Instructions." Jessica replied.

"Oh," Milo said feeling a little embarrassed. "We just call them modifications."

"I had a lady order a Caesar Salad with no cheese and no dressing," Jessica said, "and complain that it was just a big bowl of lettuce, and it was, because that is what she asked for."

"I had someone do the exact same thing!" Milo said. "I don't know what she was thinking."

"Okay," I've got the Chicken Fried Steak," a guy said as he came up to their table, putting the Chicken Fried Steak in front of Doris, and a burger medium with fries, as he put the burger and fries in front of Milo, making Milo wonder how he know who got which item.

"How did he know who had what?" Milo asked Jessica.

"We use pivot-point seating," Jessica said. "Each seat has a number so the food runner knows where it goes."

"Aha! Another difference," Milo thought.

"What do you do when people switch seats?" Milo asked.

"Oh, that," Jessica said. "We call that musical chairs. Then it's on them. Anything else I can get either of you?"

"I think we're good," Doris said.

***

"Well, this was great," Doris said, tapping Milo's left knee, but this time lifting her hand back up instead of leaving it there as she turned to Milo and he turned to her as they finished boxing up their leftovers. This time Milo couldn't help but look down at the tap, and Doris noticed his eyes move toward his knee.

"Umm," Milo said. "We're just friends, right?" knowing he liked Doris, but this was the first time he had even talked to her about anything other than work.

"Oh that. I'm just a very touchy-feely person. You're a nice guy, but I do that with a lot of people. I'm sorry if that makes you uncomfortable," she said, and leaned over and gave him a quick kiss.

"Okay," Milo said, letting his relief show, realizing that his reply could give her the impression that he didn't like her, and quickly added "I like you and this was great and I'd like to do it again, but this is the first time I've had a chance to talk to you outside of work... and all we talked about was work."

***

Milo heard some commotion, and looked over and saw Dominic and Andy pushing the tables together in The Prison. "It's all yours," Andy said as he approached Milo. You're getting a 14-top. You think you can handle it Chief?"

"14-top?" Milo asked. He had never heard that expression before.

"Yeah, a party of 14. Eight adults and six kids," Andy replied. You think you can handle it?

"Um yeah," Milo said. "Yeah, I can."

"Big check. A chance to make some more money with only two hours until closing. Easy money, he thought to himself."

"Keep control, stay organized," Carmine said as she walked by. "Try to get all the drinks first if you can. Lemme know if you need any help. You got this."

Milo could see that the 14-top took up one of the entire prison cells with the tables turned diagonally through the cell. Normally, that cell had one rectangular 4-top on the left side, and two rectangular 4-tops on the right side, with Bubba in the back left corner. The other cell was a mirror image. Turning the tables at an angle was the only way they would fit, and even then, it was tight, because in order to fit fourteen, you had to have one person on each end. He figured he would make a lot of money off of this table, which was great because his section was empty, and it would be easy money.

Through the corner of his eye he could see Dominic putting down menus at each chair, so he walked back to the prison cell to greet his guests. As Dominic finished putting the menus down, Milo saw him walk over to the front door, and lead two guests over to his 14-top.

"Welcome to prison," Milo said, as the guests approached the entrance to the cell. "I'm Milo and I'll be taking care of you tonight."

"Thank you," a man in his forties with a teenage boy who was probably a few years younger than Milo said. He stopped at the entrance and looked at the setup, and paused. "Ya know," he said, "I don't think this is gonna work." He thought for a minute and gestured to the tables. "Can we take these two tables," he began pointing to tables 46 and 47 next to the other prison cell, "and turn them so they are one long table for the adults, and then take this table, and turn it sideways?" he continued, gesturing to the left side of the cell, "and put the kids there?"

"Sure," Milo said. "But the kid's table will only fit four. They told me there were six kids."

The man paused for a minute, looked at the table, and said "Turn it sideways and put one chair on each end. They're small. They'll fit."

"I'll set that up for you." As Milo began to move the tables, the man and his teenage son began to help, and the three of them had the tables set up the way the man wanted pretty quickly.

As the man and his son sat at the far end of the long table, he said "My wife and daughter will be here soon. They'll be on my check. And the rest of the party will be here pretty soon too."

"Okay," Milo said. "Can I start you with anything to drink while you're waiting? A couple of Long Island Iced Teas, or beers," Milo asked, hoping to break the ice and hoping the two would find humor in his question since the son obviously was not old enough to drink.

"Oh," The son exclaimed. "I'll have one of those iced teas."

"You're not having one of those iced teas," the father snapped at the son. "Not for a few more years anyway. We had that discussion when I found the liquor in your Yeti."

"I didn't ask for liquor, dad," the son replied. "I asked for an iced tea."

"Well not that kind of iced tea," the dad said.

Realizing his attempt to break the ice had not gone as planned, Milo quickly added "Well, we have black tea and guava iced tea."

"I'll have black tea," the son said.

"Okay," the man said. "Bring him a black tea, and I'll start with water. In fact, just bring everyone a water to make it easy."

"Make it easy?" Milo thought. "That had not gone as planned either," knowing that bringing fourteen waters for people who might not even want them was a lot of extra work if no one ended up drinking the waters, and if people had water they were less likely to order sodas, and that could bring his check down by $30 to $40.

Milo returned to the cell with on black tea and fourteen waters, six in kid's cups with lid. Milo had learned early on that if you put kid's drinks in regular cups you end up mopping up drinks when the table leaves, and if you ask the parents if they want kid's cups or regular cups, you have at least a 50% chance of the parents choosing a regular cup for a kid who will probably end up spilling it anyway. As a few more guests arrived, Milo began putting the kid's waters on the kid's table, and the adult waters on the other table.

"Myrna," the man said to one of the guests who was just arriving. Myrna was an older woman, a little on the heavy side, and dressed a little more formally than the man and his son, so Milo figured maybe this was a family gathering or something, and maybe she was an aunt or a grandmother. But the man just called her Myrna, so maybe not. "So good to see you. Abby will be here with little Abagail soon."

"They're out in the parking lot," Myrna said. "I saw them parking."

As Myrna walked into the cell, she looked around at the cell, Bubba, and the table setup. "How cute," she said. As she was looking around, a few more guests began to filter in, and move toward the tables.

"Do you think this is going to work?" one woman asked out loud to anyone who was listening. "I mean with the two tables. Would it be better if we turned them at an angle and made it into one long table?"

The thought of moving the tables again, especially with fourteen people in the cell gave Milo a knot in his stomach, but the man who was the first to arrive spoke up. "We've got the kids at that table," pointing to the smaller table with the six kid's cups on it, and the adults over here," he said.

"Oh, okay," the woman said slowly, cupping her right hand and then rubbing one hand just below her neck, "John, they're not that small anymore. You think Justin is the only one who's growing up?" still not convinced this was the best setup.

"Hello Aunt Myrna," a woman with an eight year old girl in tow said as she greeted a kissed Myrna on the cheek. "You remember Abagail, don't you?"

"Aha," Milo thought. "This must be the wife and daughter, and it's her aunt!"

"Of course I do," Myrna replied. "My, you've gotten so big Abagail," Myrna said.

"So have you," Abagail replied, thinking she was paying her great-aunt a compliment, Abby blushing at Abagail's remark while Myrna just chuckled. "I'm eight," Abagail proudly announced.

"Well so you are," Myrna said. "So you are!"

As everyone filtered in and were saying their hellos, Milo tried to do a quick count to figure out how many were here and how many more were coming because he didn't see any kids, and he had gotten six waters in kid's cups, but people kept moving around, making it hard to count.

Noticing that the man who was first to arrive also realized the "kids" were not kids anymore, he heard the man whisper to his teenage son. "Go sit with the other teenagers," and the son walked over to the other table, high-fived a few of the other teen boys, and began to talk with them.

The man then stood up on his tip toes and tried to get everyone's attention. "Everyone," he said, but no one was listening, "Everyone," he said a little louder, which got everyone's attention. "Milo here," he said pointing to Milo, "was kind enough to set up a table for the adults," pointing to the table he was at, "and a kid's table," pointing to the other table. "Milo is going to be taking care of us tonight."

"Kids?" Abby exclaimed with a chuckle in her voice. "John, they're all teenagers now except for Abagail."

For a minute Milo felt as if he was being thrown under the bus because John had implied it was his idea to set up a kid's table for people who turned out to be almost adults and almost his age."

"Well it's a teen's table," John came back with quickly. "Let's all sit down so we can order some food, and then we can catch up with each other. Teens and Abagail at that table," John said, pointing to the smaller table, "And everyone else at this table," he said.

Milo felt vindicated by John's calling it the teen's table instead of the kid's table, but looked down at the teens crowded around the small table and the waters in kids cups and wondered how it must feel to be in your teens drinking out of a kid's cup. He kind of felt bad for the "kids" who were almost as old as he was drinking out kid cups.

Milo backed up to the entrance to the cell, to let everyone get seated, and as he backed up, Carmine walked by and tapped him on his shoulder. "Milo, I'm cut. It's just you and Christina now. I seated table 82. They asked to sit out there. And Andy just cut Dominic, so keep an eye on the door."

"Um, okay." Milo said, realizing that table 82 was one of the mall tables, wondering why the managers always cut one server and the host at the exact moment a party of fourteen was getting situated. He had never seen anyone sit at one of the mall tables before. "Um, can Christina take 82? I have this 14-top and they're just about to order."

"She said her feet are hurting her, and it's too far to walk," Carmine replied.

"What about Janice? Can she take them?" Janice had been at the restaurant for what seemed like since day one, but in reality it had just been about eight years. She was the only person who just bartended, and looked down at everyone else, including the managers, but was only nice to them because she knew that would help her manipulate them… all of the other bartenders bartended and waited tables.

"She's working on closing the bar. She said she only wants anyone who sits at the bar."

"Closing the bar? Milo asked. "We're still open for more than two hours."

"It's Janice," Carmine replied. "Your 14-top is looking at their menus. Go greet 82 now."

***

The sliding glass door felt like it weighed a thousand pounds, but Milo managed to open it, but it quickly slid closed behind him. As he approached table 82, he saw a young couple, who he guessed to be about his age, both sitting on the same side of the table.

"Hi, my name is Milo," he said as he approached the table.

No answer and no recognition that he was even there.

"Can I start you with anything to drink? A Long Island Iced Tea or a beer?"

Looking up, the man said "Yeah, I'll have one of those Long Island Iced Teas."

"Can I see your I.D. please?" Milo asked.

The woman reached in her purse and pulled out the man's I.D. and handed it to Milo. Milo looked at it. It looked like him. 2003, but as he began to hand it back to her, he pulled it back to himself to look again. "Yep, he's already had his birthday this year, so he's good to go," Milo thought to himself.

"I'll just have a Coke," she said. "I'm only twenty. I'm his trophy wife."

Milo wasn't sure if she was trying to be funny, or if she really thought a one year difference was enough to qualify her as a trophy wife. "I'll be back with your drinks in a few minutes," he said.

"Um, these cheese twigs," the man said "Is that like fried cheese?"

"It IS fried cheese," Milo said.

"How many come in an order," the man asked.

"Um, I think it's about ten or twelve," Milo said.

"You want fried cheese, baby?" the man asked the woman, who nodded affirmatively.

"Put in an order of cheese twigs," the man said, adding "with a side of ranch... extra ranch."

*** 

Milo rang in the cheese twigs and the drinks, and went back to his 14-top. "So, can I start you with some appetizers?" Milo said, looking at no one in particular.

Fourteen people and no response. "Um, some cheese twigs, spinach and artichoke dip, or Cheasy to eat Cheese Bread?" he asked.

John looked up from his menu. "Tell ya what," he said. "Put in an order of Cheasy to, uh, whatever you call it, cheese bread for this table," motioning his hand around the table in a circular motion, "uh make that two, and put in one for the kid's, uh, teen's table too. Anyone want anything else?" he asked, looking around.

"Um," said one of the teens. "I'll have this steak," pointing to the menu.

"We're just ordering appetizers right now," one of the parents chimed in, so Milo didn't write it down.

Milo looked around, and as he was about to go put the order in, he heard "Ranch, can we get some ranch with it."

Milo put the order for three Cheasy to eat Cheese Breads in and headed to the service bar, only to find the Long Island Iced Tea he had rung in not there. "Janice," he said a little tentatively because he had never actually talked to her before. "I rang in a Long Island Iced Tea."

Without saying a word, she made his Long Island Iced Tea while he poured the trophy wife's Coke, and headed off to table 82.

As he delivered the drinks, he asked, "Are you ready to order?"

"Yeah," the man said. "I want pasta. I'll have the Fiery Prawns and Pasta. Is that good?"

"One of my favorites," Milo said, looking up at the trophy wife, not even trying to be diplomatic, sensing that the 14-top was probably ready to order.

"I think I'll have the, uhhh," as she ran her right index finger down the menu.

Milo got the feeling he was going to be standing there while she read the menu. Normally he would tell her he'd give her a few minutes to look over the menu, but he knew he may be at the 14-top for a while, so he said, "Do you like pasta? Salads? Sandwiches?" trying to help her along, but he heard the sliding glass door open, looked back, and saw Andy walking up with an order of Cheese Twigs.

"Cheese Twigs," Andy said, as he put the food on the table. Looking at the woman, Andy sensed she was having trouble deciding what to order.

"Not sure what you want?" Andy asked.

"Yeah," the woman said, her voice tapering off. "I'm not sure if I want a sandwich or a salad."

"I know a sandwich that's a combination of both. Do you like wheat bread?" Andy asked her.

"Yes," the woman replied.

"Bacon?" he asked?

"Yes," the woman replied.

"How about lettuce and tomato?

"Uh yes, I do," the woman replied.

"Then I've got just the sandwich for you!" Andy said. "It comes with fries, and I'll have the chef put mayonnaise on it too. Is that okay?"

"Yes!" the woman replied, smiling for the first time. "And a side of ranch for the fries."

As Andy and Milo walked through the sliding glass door, Milo looked at Andy and said, "But that's just a BLT. You can get that anywhere."

"Make the guest feel special, and they'll be eating out of your hand. Works every time," and he paused. "Now get back out to your 14-top. I brought out their appetizers and I think they're ready to order."

"On my way," Milo said.

"And Chief," Andy said as Milo looked up. "The 14-top thinks you're great." Milo's face lit up and he got a spring in his step, as he headed toward his 14-top and Andy headed back toward the office, not having a clue about what the 14-top thought of Milo, but knowing he had just made Milo feel special.


Milo walked into the cell to see the guests at the 14-top eating their Cheasy to eat Cheese Breads. "So, are we ready to order? Milo asked.

"I think we are," John said. "I think we are," his voice tapering off. "We'll start. Honey," he said, looking at Abby, "What would you like?"

"Um, you go first. I'm still looking," Abby said.

"Okay," John said. "I'll have the 8 ounce sirloin medium well with a baked potato," he said, "with a side of ranch," he added.

Milo looked at Abby. "I'll have the Pomodoro Pasta," Abby said, "But can I add chicken to it?"

"Of course," Milo replied.

"And Abagail, what would you like?" Abby asked, looking over at the teen's table and raising her voice slightly so Abagail could hear her.

"I'll have the kid's chicken toes with a side of ranch," Abagail replied.

Milo looked at Abby's brother, and he pointed to the menu as he spoke. "Um, I'll have this steak," the teen said.

"Which one?" Milo asked, bending a little to try to see which steak he was pointing to.

"Ummm, the 22 ounce Porterhouse," the boy said.

"Justin," Milo heard Abby snap from the next table over. "You're not getting a 22 ounce steak."

"But mom," the boy who Milo now knew was named Justin said.

"Justin. Just get what your father got."

Not even knowing what his father ordered, Justin grumbled "okay," and looked back at the other teens.

"You want the baked potato too?" Milo asked.

"I guess," Justin said, quickly adding, "You got fries?"

"Yup," Milo said.

"I'll take fries... with a side of ranch," Justin said.

Unsure which way to turn, Milo looked over to the couple next to John and Abigail. The couple seemed to be a little older, although the man had obviously dyed his hair, and in an attempt to look younger, used too much black dye, which stood out like a sore thumb, and had a pot belly. The woman, probably a brunette when she was younger, had hair that was dyed platinum blond, but Milo, as much as he was not a fashion expert, could tell it had not been done professionally. "I think we're going to share the 16" pizza," the woman said. "Is pepperoni okay?" she asked, looking over to the man.

"Sure," he said. "Do you want mushrooms too?" he asked her, but from the look on her face, it was obvious she didn't.

"We can make a pepperoni pizza with mushrooms on half," Milo said.

"That works," they both replied, nodding affirmatively, almost simultaneously.

"And the boy in blue," the man said, pointing to one of the teens at the other table, "is ours," as if they owned him.

The teens were all talking again, and three of the boys were wearing blue, but noticing that their son did not realize it was his turn to order, the father said "Anthony! Whadda ya want? Tell the waiter what you want."

One of the boys in blue, the tallest one, looked up at Milo and said "I'll have the Roast Beef Sandwich with fries. Oh, and can I get a side of ranch with the fries?"

"Sure," Milo said, writing it down, and trying to squeeze it onto his pad next to his parents' order, so he would remember who had what, not sure if he should look back at the adult table, or the teen's table. He didn't have to decide.

"I'll have the spaghetti and meatballs," the boy next to him said, "but do you have that curly pasta?"

"Cavatappi?" Milo asked.

"Yeah, whatever the curly pasta is," the boy said.

Speaking half under his breath as he wrote, Milo said "ca-va-tapp-i and meat-balls." Somehow saying it helped him write it.

"No," the boy said. "I want spaghetti and meatballs, but I want the curly pasta."

"Um, okay," Milo said, a little taken aback. "Got it. And whose check are you on?"

"I'm with my parents and my sisters," the boy said as if Milo knew who was related to who.

"And who are your parents and sisters?" Milo asked.

Before anyone could answer, Milo heard "I'll have the spaghetti and meatballs too, but no meatballs. I'm his sister. Well, I'm one of them."

Looking over to the last two teens, two girls who he then realized could be twins, but probably weren't because one girl was a few inches taller than the other, Milo asked "And what would you like?"

"We're going to share the small pizza," the taller girl said. "Just cheese."

"Don't you want pepperoni?" the shorter girl asked the taller girl.

"No, I just want cheese," the taller girl said.

"We'll do pepperoni on half," the shorter girl said.

"Do you have ranch?" the taller girl asked.

But before Milo could answer, the shorter girl piped in "No, I don't want ranch!"

"It's on the side," the taller girl told the shorter girl.

Moving over at the adult table, Milo looked over at the remaining adults.

"And who's next?" Milo asked for anyone who was listening to answer.

The conversation amongst the adults continued, and no one seemed to notice Milo standing there, and no one answered. "Um, excuse me," Milo continued. "Who's next?" Milo asked again.

"Linda," one of the other adults said, and a woman with straight dishwater brown hair pulled back with a hair pull looked up.

"What kind of red wine do you have?" She asked, totally unaware that everyone was ordering food.

"Well," Milo said, "Prisoner Red Blend is our specialty wine. We also ha..."

"Sold!" the woman said before Milo could finish the list of wines. He was kind of relieved, because he knew their specialty wine, but he got kind of foggy when he had to recite any more of them.

"And what would you like to eat?" Milo asked, looking down and seeing that Linda had not even opened her menu.

"I think I'll have a salad," Linda said kind of matter-of-factly. "Just a basic salad."

"We have Adelaide's Chef Salad. It comes with our signature Thousand Island dressing" Milo interjected, sensing that he might end up reciting the ingredients of all of the salads to her if he didn't act quickly.

"I'll take it." Linda said. "I'm easy,"

"That's why I married her," the man next to her said. "I'll have the meatloaf with mashed potatoes," the man said.

As soon as the man was done speaking, the man next to him, who was a little more buttoned up and stoic, and a little younger than the rest of the adults, but by Milo's calculations, a few years older than he was said "And I'll take the Fiery Prawns with Pasta."

"And the three of you are together?" Milo asked.

"Yeah, he's ours," the man said, "or so she tells me," pointing his thumb toward Linda. "We haven't done a DNA test yet."

Although the joke was overused, the way the man said it sounded kind of funny to Milo, but he managed not to laugh, but looking at the adult son, Milo could tell he had heard his dad use the same joke in a weak attempt at humor before.

Milo looked over at Myrna. "And last but not least, what would you like, ma'am?"

"Oooohhh, he called me ma'am," Myrna said, grabbing Milo's arm and chuckling. "I like him already! Niles, it is Niles, isn't it?" Myrna asked.

"Um, it's Milo," Milo replied, wondering if the adults were her children and the teens were her grandchildren.

"I tell you what Milo," Myrna said. I want a pastrami sandwich with coleslaw on it. On pumpernickel, toasted well. Nothing else on it. You think the chef can do that?"

"I'm sure he can," Milo said. "And whose check will you be on?"

"I'll be on my own check," Myrna said. "All by myself," singing the words to the tune of Eric Carmen's 1975 hit song, which was lost on Milo, and probably the rest of the guests.

***

"I just dropped off table 82's food," Andy said, approaching Milo as he was finishing ringing in the 14-top's food. "Check on them. The guy said it was fine but was looking at his Fiery Prawns and Pasta untrustingly when I left the table."

"How is everything?" Milo asked as he approached the table.

"Why're there shrimp in my pasta?" the man asked. "All I wanted was pasta."

"It comes with it," Milo said. "It's part of the dish. Fiery Prawns and Pasta."

"Yeah, but these are shrimp. I didn't want shrimp."

"Shrimp. Prawns. They're the same thing," Milo said, realizing his tone of voice might have sounded a little defensive. Toning it down a little, Milo asked "Do you want me to get you something else?"

"Do they cost extra?" the man asked?

"The shrimp? Milo asked, dumbfounded. "No. They come with the dish. They don't cost extra."

"I guess I'll try them," the man said, still staring at his food suspiciously and twirling the pasta.

"Mine's good," the woman said.

***

"Prisoner's up" he heard Janice say as he walked back through the sliding glass doors. He was a little surprised because he had never heard her let him know his drinks were ready before, and in fact had never spoken to him before.

As Milo delivered Linda's Prisoner, he noticed that a few people had gotten up and were now talking to people at other parts of the table. A few of the teens were talking to some of the adults, and Linda was sitting at the teen's table talking with Abagail. He put down the glass of wine in front of Linda, and looked around and asked "Does anyone else want anything to drink?" turning his head as he spoke so everyone could hear him?"

"Do you still have the Raspberry Limeade?" the tall boy in the blue, who was now standing and talking to the man with the jet-black dyed hair and the platinum blond woman, asked.

"We do," Milo answered.

"I'll take one of those please," the boy responded.

"What other flavors do you have?" Justin, now standing near the entrance to the cell, talking to Linda's husband, asked.

"We have Blueberry Orangeade and Guava Lemonade," Milo replied.

"What's guava?" Justin asked, but before Milo could answer, Justin added "I'll have the Blueberry Orangeade."

Relieved that he didn't have to answer, because he too was unsure of what guava was, but made a mental not to google it later, he looked around.

"Chivas on the rocks," the stoic man said, putting his finger up in an attempt to get Milo's attention.

"May I please see your I.D.?" Milo asked, feeling funny about carding someone who he figured to be older than he was. The man pulled out his wallet, and flipped open the compartment with his driver's license. 1998, so he's 26, and realizing that it was his birthday, Milo said "Happy bi…"

But before he could finish his words, the man put his right index finger up to his pursed lips, indicating that the fact that it was his birthday was a closely-guarded secret. "So they're not here celebrating his birthday," Milo thought to himself.

As Milo left the cell, he went back to table 82, but before he could quite make it to the table, the man made a square with his hand, indicating to-go boxes, so Milo turned around, grabbed two boxes, and printed the check, $38.46 and headed back to the table and dropped the boxes. "Any dessert?" Milo asked. "We have…"

"Nah," the man said, the woman now with both her arms wrapped around his left arm, and her head resting on his shoulder. "Just the ticket."

Milo dropped the check he had printed, and said "I'll get this whenever you are ready," and headed back to the bar to get his drinks.

As he approached the cell with his drinks, Andy and Christina, who supposedly couldn't walk very far, approached from the other side of the restaurant with some of the food for his table. Dismayed, Milo noticed that although they were all sitting down, almost everyone had switched seats once again. Milo handed the Chivas on the rocks to the birthday boy, the Raspberry Limeade to the tall boy in blue, and the Blueberry Orangeade to Justin. Stepping aside, just inside the cell, Milo let Andy and Christina in with the food, though neither one of them said anything. Milo figured he need to take the lead, and looked at the items Christina, who was closest to him, was holding.

"Pomodoro Pasta with chicken," Milo said, although no one noticed the three of them were standing there with hot food, and the conversation continued. A little louder, Milo said "Pomodoro Pasta with chicken."

"Me. Oh, that's me," Abby said, still at the kid's table. As Milo took the food from Christina and put it in front of Abby, she pointed at Linda's wine and said "I'll have one of those too."

"And the Roast Beef Sandwich with Fries with a side of ranch," Milo said, taking the plate from Christina.

"Me," Anthony said, although the conversation continued as if the three of them were not there, so Milo took the plate, squeezed in, and put the plate in front of him. "Can I get some more ranch please?"

Andy slid into the cell, and as Milo looked over at him, was impressed not only that Andy had three plates on one arm, but two more fanned out in his other hand. "8 ounce Sirloin with baked potato," Andy said, but the conversation continued. A little louder and a little more assertively, Andy again said "8 ounce Sirloin with baked potato." John raised his hand, and Milo took the plate from Andy and put it in front of him.

"8 ounce Sirloin with fries with ranch," Andy said, but this time the group was almost quiet. As Justin, who was now seated next to his father raised his hand, Andy delivered the plate to him.

"And I've got the cavatappi with meatballs and the spaghetti," Andy went on.

"Uh, I had the spaghetti with meatballs with the curly pasta," the boy in blue said. Not saying a thing, Andy put the cavatappi with meatballs in front of him, and as she raised her hand, he put the spaghetti in front of his sister.

Seeing the Salad, Linda said "I have the Chef Salad." Andy put it down in front of her, and tapping on her glass of wine, she looked at Milo and said "I'll have another one of these."

As Andy backed out of the cell, the group quieted down, and Christina and Ray approached with the rest of the food. As they delivered the rest of the meals, Milo looked at Abby and said "I'll be right back with your Prisoner. Does anyone else want any more drinks?"

"I'll have one of those too," Myrna said, pointing to Linda's wine.

"So will I," said the man with jet black hair and pot belly.

"Do you just want to get a bottle, and I'll just bring three more glasses?" Milo asked, immediately regretting his suggestion, and hoping someone would say no, because he had only done wine service once before.

The guests looked at each other for a minute. "Great idea," Myrna said.

Milo went over to the POS and rang in the bottle of Prisoner, and began to divide up the checks, so he would be ready when they were ready to pay. Andy came up to him with the check from table 82 and two twenty dollar bills. Milo looked at it, disappointed, and shoved it in his pocket, and continued to divide up the checks for his party in the cell.

"Um, sirloin with baked potato, sirloin with fries, Pomodoro Pasta, kids chicken toes... that goes on one check," Milo said to himself as he tapped the items and moved them over to seat 2.

"16 inch pizza, Roast Beef Sandwich, cavatappi with meatballs, spaghetti, and the Raspberry Limeade, that goes on another check," as he tapped the items and moved them over to seat 3.

"Blueberry Orangeade," Milo thought to himself. "Who had that?" He racked his brain and remembered that the teen who ordered it was standing by the entrance to the cell when he ordered it, looked over at the party and recognized that he was one of the two first people that arrived at the restaurant, and promptly tapped the Blueberry Orangeade, and moved it over to Abby and John's check.

Unsure who had the first glass of Prisoner Red Blend, Milo looked up and tried to remember who ordered it and when. Unable to remember, Milo thought it was the woman who was sharing the pepperoni pizza with the man with the jet black hair and pot belly, and moved the Prisoner Red Blend to their check.

When he got to Myrna's, he knew it would be easy because she just had the sandwich with coleslaw on it on pumpernickel toasted well, and was just drinking water.

"Done!" Milo thought to himself, proud that he had remembered who had what, despite the musical chairs.

Milo went to the bar and got the bottle of Prisoner and 4 glasses from the bar. "Janice," he said. "I've only opened a bottle of wine once. Can I open it here and bring it to them?"

"No," she replied. "It's not that hard and they're paying a lot of money for this bottle. Present the bottle to them…"

Milo looked at her, not understanding.

"Show them the bottle," she said. "Then take the knife on your wine key, cut the wrapping around the neck of the bottle, take it off, and put the corkscrew in the cork and pull it out. Then pour a little bit of wine for whoever ordered it to taste, and if they say it's okay, pour everyone else's wine, and then pour theirs."

"But no one ordered it. I suggested it."

"Then ask who wants to taste it, and let them taste it," Janice said.

"Um, I don't have…" knowing what he was about to say, Janice took her wine key and handed it to Milo.

"Bring it back," she said.

Unable to get the bottle and four glasses into his hands, Milo grabbed a tray, put the four glasses on the tray, and set off to the cell with the bottle of wine and the glasses.

He set the tray with the glasses on table 36, just outside of the cell, walked into the cell, and Myrna looked at him, so he decided to present the bottle to her. He took the bottle, held it up high by the neck, and showed it to her.

"It's fine," she said, realizing this was his attempt to present the bottle to her. By now most of the adults were watching him.

Relieved, Milo cut the wrapper from around the neck of the wine, and to his amazement, it came right off. "Easier than I thought," Milo thought to himself.

Feeling a little more confident, he opened the wine key, twisted the corkscrew worm into the cork, and pulled.

"Pop" he heard, feeling relieved, but when he looked down at the bottle and the cork, only half of the cork had come out.

He heard a little bit of a chuckle. Sweating and unsure what to do, Linda said "It's fine honey. You have to put it in all the way, but just put it back in and try again." A few of the men and teen boys laughed a little bit, and when Linda realized what she had said, she laughed a little too, but the laughing relieved the tension.

Pressing the bottle between his side and his elbow, Milo unscrewed the broken part of the cork from the corkscrew worm, took the bottle, and removed the second half of the cork. Everyone applauded, and Milo was not sure whether to feel happy that he had succeeded the second time, or disappointed in himself that he had not succeeded the first time.

"Now who'd like to taste the wine?" Milo asked, proud of himself that he remembered that step.

"I'm sure it's fine," Linda said. "I've already had a glass. "Just go ahead and pour it."

***

Taking a break from his side work, Milo figured it was time to go back and check on the 14-top.

"Can I get a box?" someone, he was not sure who, asked as he approached the cell.

"I'll take one too," someone else said.

"Me too," someone else said.

"Um, I'll just bring a bunch of boxes," Milo interjected, and turned to get some to-go boxes.

He approached the table with a stack of boxes, and started handing them out. When he got to the man with the jet black hair who was sharing the pizza with his wife, who was now leaning back and had the I-can't-eat-another-bite look, and tried to hand him a box, he put his hand up making a "stop" motion, and said "I'm gonna finish this. You think I got this belly by not cleaning my plate?" as he patted his belly.

As he was handing out the boxes, Milo asked "Would anyone like some dessert? Possibly the "Duck My Diet I'll Try It Chocolate Cake," or the "I'll Regret It But Duck It I'm Gonna Get it Banana Split?"

"What comes with the Fuck My Diet..." Anthony started, as a few people chuckled.

"Anthony!" his mom snapped. "That's not what he said."

"He just said," Anthony went on...

Seeing he needed to intervene, Milo began, "It's a personal sized chocolate cake with four scoops of chocolate ice cream," Milo said, making the quote marks with his fingers as he said the word personal, "but it's pretty big," he went on. "It's usually enough for a few people to share."

"I'll take one of those," Anthony said.

"With four spoons," his mom quickly added.

"Does the banana split really have duck in it?" Abagail innocently asked, unaware of the issue with autocorrect when trying to type the word 'fuck."

"There's no duck in any of our desserts," Milo answered. "It's just a name."

"Mom, can I get one?" she asked her mom.

"We'll all share one," her mom said. "Just bring a bunch of spoons," she said, turning to Milo. "Maybe someone else will want some."

"Put a bunch of spoons on ours too, so everyone can have some if they want." Anthony's mom said.

"You think that's enough?" John asked.

"It should be," Milo responded. "Our desserts are pretty big."

"I'll get one of them Duck it whatever chocolate cakes," the man with the jet black hair said, now finished with his pizza. "That sounds pretty good. You wanna get a dessert, babe?" he asked, looking at his wife.

"I'm full," she said. "I can't eat anymore."

"Milo," Myrna said, holding up her empty to-go box. "Do you have a smaller box? I don't need one this big." Milo hated that request because all the to-go boxes they had in the dining room were the same size. He knew there were some smaller boxes somewhere, in the back, but he wasn't sure where.

"Sure. I'll get you one," he said.

Milo rang in the desserts, trying to remember which kid who had ordered which dessert belonged to which parent. When he got to the kitchen, he managed to find one stray small to-go box in the kitchen, and brought it out to Myrna. "Mission accomplished" he thought to himself. "That was easier than I thought."

"Can I please have one of those too?" Linda asked as soon as Milo got back to the table. "I don't have much left and I don't want to waste a big box on this," she said, pointing to the remnants of her meal.

"Sure," Milo said cheerfully, not letting his voice reflect the dread of finding another small box as easily as he found the first one.

"Milo. Your desserts are ready," Ray said as Milo came back into the kitchen to look for another small to-go box. "You don't want them to get cold."

"Thanks," Milo said. "I'll be right back for them. Um, do you know where I can find a small to-go box?"

"There should be some on the sandwich station underneath and behind the buns," Ray said.

Milo wasn't even sure where the sandwich station was, but he went around and looked where he knew the sandwiches came up in the cold window. He saw the buns, looked behind, them, and voila, he found a stash of small to-go boxes. He grabbed one and headed back out to his table to give it to Linda.

"Thanks," she said.

"Can I get a small side of ranch for my fries?" Justin asked, holding up his to-go box with only fries in it.

"Sure," Milo said, wondering why he had not asked when Linda had asked for the small box. About to ask if anyone else needed anything else before he headed back to the kitchen, he thought better of it, knowing that it could save him a trip but more likely it would open up the floodgate of requests, and also knowing he had to get his desserts out before they got cold.

As he turned to go back to the kitchen, he saw Christina, followed by Ray, walking out with his desserts. "Small miracles," He thought.

He heard a phone ring, and saw the man who was drinking Chivas reach for his phone, look at it, and quickly get up and dart out of his seat and out of the cell, and headed outside.

Milo turned around, and went back into the cell, followed by Christina and Ray, and pointed to the area where Anthony was sitting and said, "You can put one Duck My Diet I'll Try It Chocolate Cake in the middle here," and turned to the area where Abagail was sitting, and said "you can put the I'll Regret It But Duck It I'm Gonna Get it Banana Split in the middle here." And then turned and pointed toward the man with the jet black hair and said "The other Duck My Diet I'll Try It Chocolate Cake is his."

Giving them a few minutes to eat their desserts, Milo took the extra to-go boxes back to the kitchen, where Christina was wiping down the soda station.

"Did they pay?" Christina asked.

"They're eating their desserts now. I'm going to go drop their checks," Milo said, and headed back to the dining room, printed the checks, and headed back to the cell.

As Milo walked into the cell, John looked up and said "Can you bring our checks please?"

"I've got them right here," Milo said, and began to distribute them.

Why's the Cavatappi with meatballs on my check?" the man with the jet black hair and pot belly asked before Milo could finish passing out the checks.

"That goes on our check," Linda said.

"Why is the glass of wine on our check," Abby asked?

"The glass of wine goes on our check, Linda said, "How're we going to do the bottle."

"Can you divide the bottle of wine four ways?" Myrna asked Milo.

"I can't divide one item," Milo said.

"Put it on my check," John said.

"Thanks," Milo said. "I'll go fix the checks and be right back with them, noticing that the restaurant closed in just about 10 more minutes."

Milo walked back to the cell, and gave everyone their corrected checks, and as soon as he handed each person their check, each immediately handed him a credit card. Checks and credit cards in hand, Milo headed toward the POS, but as he approached the POS, he heard "Hey man!"

Milo looked up and the man about his age who had been drinking Chivas was approaching him, pulling his wallet out of his pocket. "Hey man," he said again. "I'm going to pay for this. It's my Aunt Myrna's 70th birthday, and I want to treat. That's why I didn't want anyone to know it was my birthday too."

Milo slept well that night, but was suddenly jolted awake at 2:00 AM by a mysterious force previously unknown to him. "Shit!" he thought. "I never brought out that extra side of ranch to-go."

***

It had been another busy night and the restaurant, but the night was winding down and Milo and Maria were the only two servers left on the floor. There was one table seated in the restaurant, and it was Maria's, and the two of them were rolling silverware. Dominic was at the front restocking the host/hostess station. They had a lot of silverware left to roll when they ran out of napkins.

Milo looked in the cabinet below and did not see any napkins.

"I'm going to go get some more napkins from Dry Goods," Milo said.

He got to dry goods and began to look for napkins. Dry goods was a long, narrow room, but wide enough for two people to pass each other easily. The shelves were labeled, but things had been moved around so much, and the managers had not taken the time to relabel all the shelves, so the labels did not always match what was on the shelves. He found a label for napkins, but found straws on the shelf, but grabbed a box of straws to bring out to the dining room just in case they needed them. As he looked for napkins, the door opened and Dominic walked in.

"Sup bro," Dominic said.

Milo began to wonder if that was Dominic's entire vocabulary, so he just instinctively replied with "Sup," even though that was not a word he normally use.

Dominic walked past Milo and climbed up on one of the metal shelves, the metal shelf leaning forward a little as Dominic climbed up on it, grabbed a bag of Starlight mints, leaned over a little bit, and grabbed a box of wrapped toothpicks. As he grabbed the toothpicks he noticed Milo looking around. "Whatcha looking for, bro?" Dominic asked, still hanging from the shelf.

"Napkins," Milo said. "I can't find them."

"To your right, up one shelf bro," Dominic said as he jumped down.

As Milo moved to the right and reached up for the napkins, Dominic headed toward the door. As Milo was reaching up and Dominic was walking toward the door, Milo felt something brush his backside. Unprepared for this, Milo thought how odd it was, since the room was wide enough for two people to pass each other. Instinctively, Milo turned and looked. As Dominic opened the door to leave, he looked back, and gave Milo a crooked little smile. Milo's heart began to beat a little more rapidly as he tried to figure out what had just happened, feeling it was more than just an innocent brush. He tried to get it out of his mind, grabbed the napkins and looked at his watch. "Only 18 more minutes until close and I'm outta here," he thought to himself, still jittery from what he told himself had to be an accidental touch.

As he left Dry Goods, walked through the kitchen and into the dining room, Milo was surprised to see four people... two adults, and two teenagers standing at the host/hostess station. Surprised to see anyone coming in at that time of night, Milo just said "Hi." He looked around and saw that Maria's table had left and had been cleared, and Maria was nowhere in sight.

"Hi," the man said. "Table for four."

"Uh sure," Milo said, setting down the napkins and straws, and grabbing 4 menus. "Right this way," he said, motioning them to come with him.

As the party was sitting down, Milo offered them some drinks.

"We'll just start with four waters," the lady said. "We'll take a few minutes to look over the drinks.

"A few minutes," Milo thought. "We're about to close."

Milo got the waters and when he got back with them, the lady said "I'll have a glass of Chardonnay."

"Anyone else," Milo asked?

"What kind of beer do you have on draft?" the man asked.

"Uh, we have Budweiser, Rustfield Red Lager..." Milo began.

"I'll have the Rustfield Red Lager," the man interrupted.

"And for either of you?" Milo asked the teenagers.

"I'll have a Coke," the teen boy said.

"And I'll have a Shirley Temple with 4 cherries," the teen girl said.

"Okay," Milo said. "I'll be right back with your drinks," not quite sure how he was going to get the wine and beer since there was no one on the bar. "Were you ready to order?"

"Not yet," The woman said. "We need a few minutes... but put in an order for the spinach and artichoke dip to get us started."

"Absolutely," Milo said, knowing that this was not a quick item, because it had to bake. Turning away, Milo heard the woman begin to say something. Milo turned back toward the table.

"Ya know, we just got in from Springfield. Such a long drive… we're all exhausted and hungry. We just needed somewhere to eat and relax, but we couldn't find anywhere open and were surprised to find you were still open. I'm so glad you're still open."

Knowing what he really wanted to say, but couldn't, Milo simply said "I'm glad you found us." Feeling as if he didn't want to make them feel rushed, he sensed the woman wanted to tell him more. But not really caring about what she probably wanted to tell him and not wanting to prolong the niceties, but trying to be polite, Milo added "So what were you doing in Springfield?"

Milo braced himself for a long drawn out answer that he really didn't want to hear, but instead the woman just said "Oh, just visiting some family we hadn't seen for a while. It was so good to see them."

Relieved that the woman gave a quick answer, Milo said "It's always great to be able to visit with family." He paused. "Let me go get your appetizer started and get your drinks."

"Andy, I need some drinks," Milo said as he walked into the office.

"You have a table?" Andy asked. Then Andy realized it was a dumb question and got up to get the drinks.

As Andy poured the wine and the beer, Milo dug around in the refrigerator for the grenadine and the cherries. With cherries and grenadine in one glass, Milo pressed both glasses up against the levers to dispense the respective sodas.

Milo heard a hissing sound, and felt a sticky spray of liquid come at him from both sides, covering his shirt in syrup and soda water.

Milo heard a loud chuckle from Andy, who was usually pretty stone-faced and even-keeled. "Nozzles are off," Andy said to Milo, unable to control his laughing.

"Yeah, I figured it out," Milo laughed, wiping himself off.

Still sticky and wet, Milo put the drinks on a tray and began to walk toward the table. "Have they ordered yet?" Andy asked.

"Just the spinach and artichoke dip," Milo replied.

"Try to get them to order when you go back with the drinks," Andy said.

As he walked toward the table, Milo heard Ray call from the kitchen "spin dip is up." A few moments later, Ray arrived at the table with the spinach and Artichoke Dip at the same time Milo arrived with the drinks. The kitchen staff usually did not run food, but Milo knew that with 4 minutes until close, Ray wanted to get this table out of there as much as Milo did.

"Spin Dip," Ray said as he put the spinach and artichoke Dip on the table. Normally Milo would have been annoyed at someone using restaurant jargon with a guest, but at this time of night he didn't care.

Milo delivered the drinks and asked, "So, what can I get you?" Usually he would have asked if they were ready or if they wanted more time, but he wanted to move them along without rushing them.

"I think we will each have a burger," the man said, moving his hand back and forth between him and his son. "Medium,' he added.

"No, I want mine rare," the son chimed in.

"That's going to be red in the middle," the father said to his son.

"I know. That's how I like it," the son said indignantly.

"Okay, rare it is," the father said, "but just for his," he added. "I want mine medium."

"And what would you like?" Milo asked the mother and daughter.

"I'll have the tuna salad platter," the mother said."

"I'll have the same as her," the daughter said.

"Easy enough," Milo thought, because he knew the tuna platters were premade and would be easy for Ray, but then the mother interjected.

"But tell the chef…" Milo had grown to hate that expression because he knew they had line cooks and not chefs and that although Ray was great at executing the items on the menu, he couldn't create a dish from scratch to save his life. "That I would like mine with extra sliced tomatoes and cucumbers instead of the potato salad."

"And for yours?" Milo asked the daughter.

"I'll take mine the way it comes," she said.

"Umm, okay," Milo said, as he wrote the order down on his pad. "Anything else" Milo asked, praying that they would say no. They looked at each other, and no one said a word, so Milo took that as a no.

***

"Hey Ray," Milo said, walking into the kitchen. "I just rang in their order, noticing that Ray was sliding two pre-made tuna salad platters that he thought were not going to get sold into to-go boxes for himself and his girlfriend.

Ray took the check off of the printer, read it, turned the grill back on, and threw two hamburger patties on the grill.

Realizing that Ray had been wrapping up two tuna salad platters that he thought would not be sold to take home for himself and his girlfriend, Milo watched Ray take the two tuna salad platters he had just slid into to-go boxes and slide them back onto plates, removing the lettuce underneath one of them, along with the potato salad that sat on the lettuce into the garbage, and replace that portion of lettuce with fresh lettuce, sliced tomatoes, and cucumbers.

***

It had been about 20 minutes since Milo delivered the food and refreshed the drinks. Everyone had eaten about half of their meals, and they were just chatting.

"How are we doing over here?" Milo asked. "Ready for dessert?" We have the …"

"Oh, no dessert," the mother said, looking at the rest of the family for confirmation.

"Then should I bring you some boxes?" Milo asked.

They all looked at each other, and the mother replied, the words coming out slowly, "Oh, I don't know. We're still nibbling and chatting. We're still trying to unwind."

"Nibbling? Chatting? Unwind?" Milo thought. "We've been closed for thirty-five minutes and they want to nibble, chat and unwind?"

"But, bring us four boxes," the father interjected.

Milo went and got four to-go boxes and handed them to the son, who was closest to him. The son handed them to his father, who took them, and set them down in a pile at the far end of the table.

"Are they still here?" Andy asked as Milo walked back into the office.

"Yeah," Milo said, noticing the drawer to one of the filing cabinets was open, and Andy had a pile of yellowing booklets and papers spread out over the counter in the office.

"Did you drop the check?" Andy asked.

"They're not even done eating," Milo said. "I got them to-go boxes, and they took them, and put them on the far end of the table and continued talking."

"What are you doing?" Milo asked, pointing at the pile of yellowing booklets and papers.

"Cleaning out the filing cabinet," Andy replied. "Figured it was a good time to do it since I'm stuck here. It hasn't been cleaned out in years."

Milo moved a little closer and started looking at the booklets Andy had spread out.

**Visit Bubba in Prison Employee Handbook 1992**, Milo saw on one of the booklets, with a picture of their building, but no mall.

"That's our building, but where's the mall?" Milo asked.

"Wasn't built yet," Andy replied. "They built the mall around the building."

"When did they build the mall?" Milo asked, remembering that Sandy had said something about this when she was training him.

"Dunno," Andy said. "Maybe mid to late 90s. I wasn't here then."

Milo started flipping through the handbook, reading some of procedures.


**Changing Dirty Ashtrays**

1. **Get a clean ashtray to replace the dirty ashtray.**
2. **Place the clean ashtray upside down, directly on top of the dirty ashtray. The dirty ashtray is now covered with the clean ashtray.**
3. **Lift both ashtrays away from the table. This way, the cigarette ashes won't blow onto the table or on the guest.**
4. **Place the clean ashtray on the table.**


"Changing dirty ashtrays?" Milo asked Andy. "Why would you have ashtrays in a restaurant?"

Taken aback, Andy looked up and realized Milo was serious. "You used to be able to smoke in restaurants," he said, "but only in the smoking section."

"Where was the smoking section?" Milo asked.

"Dunno," Andy replied. "Probably the tables near the bar."

"Well what kept the smoke only in that area?" Milo asked.

"Nothing. It got into the whole restaurant. I remember coming in every morning to the restaurant I worked at back then, and the whole restaurant had the smell of stale smoke. That's how I knew I was in the right place."

Just then Milo heard the front door open. He went out to the front of the restaurant and saw a Door Dash delivery person standing there. "Hi," Milo said, approaching the man. Instead of responding, the man lifted his phone up, shoved it in Milo's face, almost hitting Milo in the face in the process.

Milo saw that the order was an order of Fiery Prawns and Pasta and a Meatloaf Sandwich with fries for Sharon. He went to the to-go area and saw two to-go boxes there, both of which had condensation on the inside of the clear plastic lid. As he opened each of the boxes to make sure the order was correct, the condensation dripped down from the inside of the lids into the food. The Fiery Prawns and Pasta looked alright, although a little dried out, but the bread on the meatloaf sandwich was dried out and the fries were shriveled up. He looked at the time on the ticket, and it read 8:33 PM, more than two hours earlier. Unsure what to do, he bagged the food up and handed it to the Dasher, wishing him a good night, as the man left without saying a word.

Milo looked over at his table and it looked as if they may be ready to go. He printed out the check, and headed over to check on his guests. As he approached, he saw they were boxing up their food.

"Can I have a side of ranch for this?" the mother asked, pointing to her salad.

"Me too," the daughter said.

"Sure," Milo said, "I'll just leave this for when you're ready," dropping the check, and headed back into the kitchen and to expo. He opened up the refrigerator where they kept pre-poured sauces and dressings for to-go orders, and he saw ketchup, Bleu Cheese, Italian, Thousand Island, but no Ranch.

"Shit," he thought, grabbing two to-go ramekins and lids, made a beeline for the walk-in, and filled the to-go ramekins from the store and pour.

Hearing the door open as Milo exited the walk-in, Andy called down the hall, "They gone yet?"

"I'm getting them to-go ranches. I already dropped the check," Milo answered.

When he got back to the table, they had all boxed up their food, and he handed the women their ranches. He looked at the table for the check but didn't see it.

"Would you like four waters to-go?" Milo asked, trying to think of something to say to prompt them to pay the check, or for a reason to come back to the table.

Looking at each other, the father said "Um, no, not to go, but if you could refill these waters," pointing to the cups on the table, "that would be great."

"It's going to be a long night," Milo thought to himself.

\*\*\*

It was the busiest Saturday night at the restaurant Milo had seen. The mall was holding an indoor concert in the former food court, and from the noise coming from that direction, Milo sensed that it was packed and people were having a good time, and the crowds of people walking through the mall gave Milo a sense of what the dying mall felt like back in its heyday. Mall management had let the restaurant know in advance, so Andy scheduled ten servers, two bartenders, two bussers, three host/hostesses, himself, and the manager trainee, Amanda. They had been on a one-hour wait for parties of two to four, and a two-hour wait for larger parties. It was the first time Milo had seen servers scheduled for the mall tables, and one of the few times Milo had seen servers scheduled in the prison cells, and each server had four or five tables. Milo had tables 63, 64, 65, and 66, the latter of which is in the prison cell.

Milo noticed that Sabrina's two tables in the prison cell, 56 and 57 had been empty for a while, and that his table 66, which was just finishing their dinner, had been the only table seated in the cell for about 15 minutes. As soon as table 66 paid, and Milo went to collect the credit card slip, Nathan, the busser, and Dominic rushed in to clear the table as quickly as possible. Thinking, this was odd, but appreciated, Milo was at first impressed but his heart quickly sank when he saw them turning all three tables in the cell at an angle and positioning them into one long table. He knew that because two of the tables were Sabrina's, she would get the party.

"Bro," Dominic said and paused, as if he was trying to remember what he was going to say next, and then snapping his fingers to help himself remember. "Sabrina's getting a 12-top in the cell. She's using one of your tables, so Andy said you'd get her next table when they leave and it gets seated again."

Unsure which tables besides the two in the cell were Sabrina's, Milo looked around, and saw that the restaurant was full, there were several 4-tops throughout the restaurant that had been pushed together to accommodate large parties, and not only was the bar three deep, but people were clustered around the high-tops, and people who could not find a space at the high-tops had just gotten their drinks from the bar and were spread out in between and around the high tops, and abutting up to table 76, the first and only table after the high tops, and no one looked as if they were in a hurry to leave. A little disappointed but realizing he had no choice, he simply said "okay."

As Milo looked up, he saw one of the four women at table 65 gesture for him to come over. Noticing that their plates all had just a little bit of food left on them, Milo asked, "Would you like to-go boxes for these?"

They all looked at each other, somehow able to communicate to each other without speaking, and one of the women said, "No, I don't think so. I think we're done."

"Sure," Milo said, reaching over to stack and clear the plates and silverware. He wanted to get as much off of the table as quickly as he could so he could get it reseated again as soon as possible when the women got up.

As Milo was lifting up the stack of dirty plates, Nathan swooped in. "I'll get those," Nathan said, taking the plates from Milo.

"Would anyone like any dessert?" Milo asked. "We have Duck…"

As he was asking, the four women looked at each other, and the same woman said "No," and then paused. "Wait, what? You have duck for dessert?"

"No," Milo said smiling. "Those are the names of our desserts. We have Duck My Diet I'll Try It Chocolate Cake and I'll Regret It But Duck It I'm Gonna Get it Banana Split," Milo said.

The women all chuckled a little bit, but again they looked at each other, and the same woman said, "No. If I eat anything else you'll have to roll me out of here," as if Milo had never heard that one before.

"Thank you god," Milo thought, wanting to get them cashed out and get the table turned as quickly as possible, but instead he just said, "I understand. I'll be right back with the check."

"Oh, we're on one check," one woman said, raising her right index finger, and motioning it back and forth between her and the woman next to her, "and they're on one check," pointing to the other two women.

As soon as the women left, Milo stacked and cleared the remaining plastic tumblers from the table, and prepared to head back to dish, but once again,

Nathan, bored because the tables were not turning quickly, swooped in, grabbed them from Milo, and said "I'll get those for you buddy," and took the tumblers and left.

As Milo turned to get a towel from the sanitizer bucket to wipe the table, a group of four guys who had been standing along the wall between tables 75 and 76, talking to their friends at table 75, dashed over, drinks in hand and sat themselves at the table.

Feeling as if he had just been punched in the stomach, Milo was not sure which way to turn or what to do, but fortunately he didn't have to decide. Walking over with the tablet with the waiting list and seating chart, Amanda approached the table.

"Hi guys," Amanda started, the four of them looking up at her as he began to speak. "Unfortunately we're on a wait right now, so we have people waiting for this table."

"We're on the waiting list," one of the guys responded defensively. "Steinman," he said. "Take a look."

Amanda looked down at the tablet, scrolled a little bit, and said "We still have two parties waiting ahead of you."

"But these are our friends," the guy at the table said, pointing to table 75. "You mean with all of these tables in the restaurant," he began, as he motioned his hand through the air, as if to swoop it throughout the entire restaurant, "you can't give them one of these tables?"

Looking around, Amanda saw a few tables starting to clear out. "Sure guys. Enjoy your meal."

"Thanks," the guy said in a tone of voice that made Milo feel as if the guy wouldn't have given in if Amanda hadn't relented.

Walking away, Amanda motioned for Milo to come with him, so Milo walked with her. "You can still get them their meals," Amanda said. "Go grab four menus from the front and bring them to them."

As Milo returned with four menus, he offered them to the guys, none of them paying him much attention. Finally one of the guys looked up and said "We're just going to have drinks for now, but pausing and then adding, "But leave one menu." Pausing again, he looked at Milo and asked, "What's a good appetizer to share?"

"Well," Milo said, "A lot of people share the Gotcha Nachos, or the Cheasy to Eat Cheese Bread, or…"

"We'll have an order of those nachos," the same guy said, cutting Milo off mid-sentence.

"It comes with your choice of toppings. What would you like on them?" Milo asked. Sensing the guy was unsure, he continued, "Beef, cheese, tomatoes, jalapenos, sour cream?"

"All that sounds good," the guy said. "Oh, and we have a tab at the bar. Steinman. Tell the bartender to put them on our tab."

Once again deflated, Milo could barely speak. "Okay," he said starting to walk away.

"Oh," the guy said. "Tell the bartender to bring another round," pointing at and circling the drinks with an air circle with his index finger, "and tell him to put it on our tab."

With effectively only two tables for the time being, 63 and 64, both of which were taking their sweet time eating, Milo went up to the host/hostess station and looked at the tablet with the floor plan to see which other tables were in Sabrina's section, so he would know which table he could have to make up for her using his table in the cell. As he looked, he saw that she had tables 54 and 55, but 53 and 54, both rectangular 4-tops, were pushed together for a party of six that Carmine had taken, and still had unopened birthday presents sitting on one end of the table. So table 55 it would be. That would be his table.

\*\*\*

"Can you help me carry these drinks?" Sabrina asked Milo as he was at the soda station restocking plastic tumblers. Looking down, he saw 2 trays, one with 12 waters and one with an assortment of sodas and drinks from the bar.

"Okay," he said, as he followed her with the tray of waters, while she carried the sodas and bar drinks. As they got to the cell, they both squeezed in to distribute the drinks, the distribution of the waters going much faster than the bar drinks and sodas.

"Can we get some silverware?" someone asked, looking at Milo.

"And some extra napkins," someone else added.

"Sure," Milo said.

"We don't have any straws," someone said.

"I'll get those too," Milo said.

"Great," he thought, as he walked out of the cell. "Not only did I give her one of my tables, but now I'm waiting on it for her too."

But as he walked back toward the cell, supplies in hand, Milo saw a light at the end of the tunnel. Table 55 had left, and Nathan and Dominic were clearing off the plates, plastic tumblers, silverware, and napkins. Andy walked up with a towel in his hand, and wiped the table, and almost in rhythm, Doris approached the table, four menus in hand, followed by four people.

As Milo went into the cell to deliver the silverware, napkins and straws, Sabrina came in with two orders of Cheasy to eat Cheese Bread, a spinach and artichoke dip, followed by Carmine who was carrying two orders of wings. Milo left the cell to go to the server station, to grab some silverware. As he turned around and approached the table, his heart sank once again. Sabrina came out of the cell and immediately darted to table 55.

"Hi, my name is Sabrina, and I'll be taking care of you tonight," Milo heard her say, as he turned and went back to the server station to return the silverware."

"Sabrina," Milo said, as she got to the server station to ring in the drinks for table 55. "That's supposed to be my table since you have my table 66."

"But then I'll only have 1 table because Carmine has 54 for her 6-top," Sabrina said. You have three other tables.

"But your table is a 12-top," Milo said, "and you're using one of my tables for it. And no I don't because 65 seated themselves at my table and is ordering from the bar."

"Well you still have two tables and with 55 I have two tables, so we're even," she reasoned, her flawed logic not registering with Milo.

"Just take one of Carmine's tables because she has one of mine," Sabrina responded, unrelenting and unapologetic, and walked toward the kitchen.

*** 

Milo went up to the host/hostess station, looked at the tablet, and saw that table 50 was one of Carmine's tables. Through the corner of his eye, Milo saw Sabrina approach table 50, which was not her table and not even near her section. As Carmine happened to walk by, Milo asked "Why did you give 50 to Sabrina?"

"I have one of her tables, so I am giving her one of mine," Carmine responded. "That's the way we do it. It's only fair."

"Yeah, but she has one of mine, but I didn't get one of hers, so she told me to take one of yours," Milo responded.

A little baffled and trying to decipher what Milo had just said, Carmine looked at Milo. "Well why didn't you just take one of hers?" Carmine asked. "If you had done that you wouldn't be in this situation," effectively blaming Milo for not making it to table 55 before Sabrina did.

"Because," he started, raising his voice a little, but then realizing that his frustration was coming through in his tone of voice. "I couldn't because by the time I got to her table, she had already greeted it," he said, toning his voice down a little, realizing that explaining it to Carmen would not change anything.

"Well that's between you and her," Carmine said, walking away.

As Milo approached Sabrina at the server station, he began to speak. "You told me to take Carmine's next table since she has one of your tables and you have one of my tables, but I don't have one of your tables," realizing that his attempt to reason with her was probably all in vain.

"Okay," Sabrina said. "Then take table 50. All I did was get them four waters," she said. "They haven't ordered anything yet."

"Well that was easier than I thought," Milo said to himself, as he headed off to table 50.

As Milo approached table 50, he noticed that it was a party of two girls and two guys, probably about his age.

"Hi," Milo said. "My name is Milo. Are you ready to order?" he asked.

"I have a question," one of the guys asked. "This Ice Cream Mundae, can we get it today even though it's not Monday?"

"Yeah," Milo responded. "You can get it any day. That's just a name," hoping they didn't order one because it was the only item on the menu that he had to make completely by himself.

"Okay, then I'll get one of those," the guy said.

"Okay," Milo said, writing it down, but a little disappointed because the desserts were all only about $8 each, but four desserts were better than nothing. "And what else?" he asked, looking around at whoever would answer.

"Four spoons," one of the girls said. "We're going to share."

As he delivered the Ice Cream Mundae with four spoons, the guy who ordered it said "Uh, can you bring us the check please? We want to get back to the concert."

"Sure," Milo said.

He printed the check and dropped it at the table, and headed off to check on his two remaining tables. The couple at 63 was on a date, leaning toward each other and each holding a glass of wine, their eyes locked as they talked, unaware of anyone around them. Milo noticed their empty plates pushed to the far side of the table, but could not reach them and did not want to interrupt them to try to clear the plates. The group of four at table 64, had been done eating for a while, nursing their almost-full drinks, chatting, and catching up. He looked up at the group at table 65, which had now grown to seven people, and who had pulled up chairs from who-knows-where, and was crammed around the 4-top, drinking, talking and laughing, and eating the remnants of the order of nachos. He then glanced over at Sabrina and Carmine delivering the food to Sabrina's 12-top in the cell. As he walked by table 65, one of the guests picked up the almost-empty plate from the nachos, handed it to Milo, and said "Hey bro, could you take this for us?" Squeezing by, Milo almost bumped into another two guests, each with three drinks in one hand and one in the other, heading over from the bar toward table 65. As they got to the table, the other guests cheered, and the two guys with the drinks in hand squeezed in, still standing up, and began to distribute the drinks to the other guests.

Now not able to get by, Milo turned around. Noticing that the guests at table 50 had left, he headed in that direction. When he got to table 50, it had been cleared and wiped, except for the check for $8.64 for the Ice Cream Mundae and a ten dollar bill.

He looked back, and saw Dominic talking to the four adults at table 64. "I was just there," Milo thought. "Why didn't they ask me for the check, or whatever they wanted when I was there?" He saw them stand up as Dominic turned around, and follow him, drinks in hand, as he led them to table 82. As they got up, the group at table 65, which had now grown to nine, got up. "Finally!" Milo thought. "Now I'll get my tables back." The group all backed away from the table a little bit, turned the table 90 degrees, moved over to table 64, still with a few water cups and a little bit of silverware on it from the party that had just moved to table 82, turned the table 64 ninety degrees, pushed the two tables together, and sat back down.

"Bro they said your party at, uh, what's that table, uh 65 was too loud." Impressed that Dominic was able to complete his sentence without pausing after the word "Bro," Milo headed over to table 82 to check on them.

Noticing that the drinks they had been nursing for what seemed like an hour were almost empty, Milo asked if anyone needed any more drinks.

"No," several people said as they shook their heads.

"We're fine," one woman said. "We're just catching up. We haven't seen each other in years," as if Milo cared.

"Okay. Well let me know if you want anything else," Milo said, turning and starting to walk away.

As Milo headed through the first sliding door back into the main part of the restaurant, Logan approached him. Logan was new, having just started a few weeks after Milo started, but had a somewhat aggressive personality, sometimes acting as if he owned the restaurant.

"What were you doing at my table?" Logan asked.

"They moved from table 64 because it was too loud," Milo told Logan.

"Well then transfer them to me," Logan said.

"They already had dinner," Milo said. "I took care of them. I'm not transferring them to you."

"Well then I get your next table," Logan said, and walked away.

Milo waited a few seconds, continued to walk toward the front of the restaurant, and noticed that table 50 had just been sat with two couples. Looking around, he noticed that Carmine still had one of Sabrina's tables for her 6-top, and Sabrina still had one of his tables in the cell for her 12-top, so Milo picked up four sets of silverware, and went up to table 50.

"Hi, my name is Milo and I'll be taking care of you tonight," he said as he put the silverware down on the table. Can I start anyone off with anything to drink, a Long Island Iced Tea, Bloody Mary, glass of wine?"

"What kind of wine do you have?" one of the men asked.

Still hating that question, but now having learned a few more wines and feeling armed with information, Milo began, "Well our specialty wine is Prisoner Red Blend…"

"Oh, I love that wine," one of the women interjected before Milo could finish. "Let's get a bottle of that she said," but remembering there were three other people with her, looked around at the other guests for confirmation. All three nodded in agreement, and she continued, "Yeah, let's get a bottle of that."

"This surf and turf," one of the men began, "Can you get any steak with the lobster?"

"You sure can," Milo said, feeling as if his night was starting to get better, noticing that all four guests were looking at the steaks.

"And if I want to substitute the lobster for a fish filet, can I do that?" the man asked.

Never having been asked that before, but not seeing why you couldn't, Milo thought for a moment, and said "I don't see why not."

Looking back at him, the man laughed a little bit and said "I'm just kidding. I'm going to get the lobster."

Milo laughed a little too, thinking that not only did he have a table that was going to have a large check, but that they were going to be a fun table, and said "I'll go get your wine and be back shortly."

As Milo turned away and headed toward the service bar, he heard "Milo," in a tone that reminded him of his father's voice when Milo had done something wrong.

Milo looked up and saw Andy standing at the service bar "Why did you take Carmine's table?"

"Because Carmine has one of Sabrina's tables, and Sabrina has one of my tables. Milo responded."

"But you already took that one 4-top at 50," Carmine said as she walked up behind him.

"But, you and Sabrina are still taking up my tables," Milo said, proud of himself that he was finally standing up for himself.

"They've been here forever," Carmine said. "I already dropped the check, and Sabrina's table is finishing up too," unsure that just because she had dropped the check, the table would be leaving any time soon.

"Milo," Andy said. "Just let her have her table. You'll be getting your tables back soon. And 63 just asked me for their check, so I'll make sure Dominic seats it as soon as they get up," as he walked away.

Milo really had come to like Andy, but knowing that Andy had made the wrong decision, he looked at Carmine and said "They want to start with a Bottle of Prisoner Red Blend," and walked away.

Andy was right about table 63. As Milo walked back toward the back of the restaurant, he saw the guests at 63 getting up to leave. As they passed Milo, the guy say "Money's on the table, dude."

"Thanks," Milo said, and headed to the table to get the money, trying to figure out how to keep the crowd that had commandeered tables 64 and 65 from taking this table too. Fortunately they seemed oblivious to the fact that this table was now empty too. As Milo took the money and the wine glasses, and headed to the bar to drop the glasses, Nathan wiped the table down, and Dominic approached the table with two guests.

"That's my table, man," Logan, who was now standing at the service bar, said to Milo as Milo dropped the wine glasses off.

"Fine," Milo said, feeling it wasn't even worth the fight, and realizing that even though Andy had done the wrong thing by giving table 50 back to Carmine, he couldn't do that to Logan, as much as he really didn't like Logan. And besides, it was starting to slow down a little and Milo wasn't even sure if they were on a wait anymore.

*** 

"I just did cuts," Amanda said as she came up to Milo in the kitchen. "Take a look at the new floor plan. Your section has changed, and you have a few more tables."

"Thanks," Milo said.

Before he could even turn around, Milo heard a voice behind him say "I'm cut. I transferred table 63 to you. I already got them drinks and put their food in."

"Thanks Logan," Milo said, as he turned around.

"Can I get a follow," Carmine said to anyone who was listening.

"Sure," Logan said, as he walked over toward expo and helped her carry two Surf 'n Turfs with an 8 ounce Sirloin and lobster tail, a Surf and Turf with 12 ounce Ribeye and six Prawns, and 22 ounce Porterhouse. Milo had no doubt where that order was going.

"I have the bottle of Prisoner you rung in," Amanda said, coming out of Dry Goods, seeing that she and Logan were just about to head toward the dining room with the meals. "I'll leave it at the bar. Make sure they're not drinking too much. This is their third bottle."

"Logan," you're up, Milo heard Tyler call from expo.

"Is that table 63?" Milo asked.

"Uh, yeah, it is," Tyler said, looking at the check.

"I'll take that," Milo said. "Logan transferred that table to me."

As he got to the table with a pizza and a salad, Milo saw a couple he figured to be about his age. "Okay, I've got a Sausage and Pepperoncini pizza," Milo said, putting the pizza on the pizza rack, "and the Cremini Salad. Who had the salad?"

"Uh, I did," the woman said a little tentatively, both of them looking at him with suspicion.

Feeling a little uncomfortable the way they were looking at him, Milo asked "Is there anything else I can get you?"

"What's this on my pizza?" The guy asked.

"Uh, pepperoncini and sausage," Milo replied.

"I ordered a sausage and pepperoni pizza," the guy said I don't even know what these little peppers are doing here."

Without missing a beat, the woman asked "And what salad is this?"

"It's the Cremini Salad," Milo replied.

"I didn't order a Cremini Salad," she said. "I ordered the Carnegie Salad."

*** 

The night was winding down, but there was still more than an hour left before closing. Milo could still hear one of the bands playing, but there were fewer people wandering through the mall, and Milo noticed that there were visibly fewer tables seated in the restaurant. The group that had orchestrated what Milo had begun to think of as a hostile takeover of tables 64 and 65 had left, but not without leaving cocktail glasses, beer glasses, beer bottles, four stacks of about five shot glasses each, several plates from appetizers, and a collection of napkins and silverware, all from items they had ordered from the bar and brought over themselves, on the table. This was in addition to the mess on the floor, which included napkins, silverware, a broken glass, and cakes of mud that had fallen from the construction boots a few of the guys were wearing.

As Milo was clearing the table, he could hear Sabrina laughing and joking with the 12-top in the cell, enjoying the rapport she had built with them, as she cleared away a few appetizer plates… or what she considered to be pre-bussing. After all, she had bussers, so why did she need to clear away their dinner plates?

As Sabrina came out of the cell with a few used appetizer plates, Nathan was passing by, and took the plates from her. She turned to Milo and said "I just love these people! They are so much fun," and turned around and went back in the cell. She pulled the check out her server book and laid it on the table and said "I'll get this whenever you are ready."

"Oh," one of the men said. "We need separate checks. "Can you please divide it up by family?" and handed the check back to her, as if she was supposed to know who was part of which family.

"Okay," Sabrina said, a little taken aback. "I just need to know who is with who so I can divide it up."

Milo could tell that Sabrina's love for the party and their love for her had faded, and the rapport she had built was starting to erode. It was now time for business and the financial transaction, and things had changed. A little annoyed, the man began, "It's me and my wife, and our three kids," pointing in the general direction of three of the kids at the table, "It's them," he continued, pointing at a couple sitting across the table from each other near the middle of the table, and their son Jacob," pointing in the general direction of another kid, "and those two and their kids," pointing to a couple at the other end of the table with two kids.

"Okay," Sabrina said. "Let me write this down, so I know who had what and who is with who, so I can divide it up." Milo sensed correctly that Sabrina did not want to go through the entire order again, but had no choice.

"Okay," the man said, a little exasperated.

Milo continued to clear the tables, listening to Sabrina and the 12-top rehash the entire order again, hoping Nathan, who had been so on his game all night would swing by to help.

"Nathan's cut," Amanda said as she walked by, and looking down at the floor underneath the table added, "And make sure you mop the floor under the table after you sweep it."

As Milo was finishing clearing the table, Sabrina had finished dividing up the check, and passed out the three checks to her party.

"Why is there gratuity on here?" another man asked, as he looked at his check.

"We add gratuity to parties of six or more," Sabrina said. It says it near the front door and on our menu."

"We're not a party of six or more," the man said. "They're five," he said pointing to the first family, "we're three, and they're four," he said turning to the other family. "Pretty simple."

"The entire party is a party of twelve, so we add gratuity," Sabrina said.

"I don't care about the entire party," the man said, "I care about..."

Walking by, Andy heard what was going on and stepped into the cell. "Sir," he said in low, calm voice. "You're not required to pay the gratuity we add on. It's just a suggested gratuity, and it even says that right here," as he pointed at the wording at the bottom of the check. "I know you would never do this, but we do have guests who feel it's alright not to take care of their server after their server has taken care of them. But we can't add it for some and not for others."

Although Milo felt Andy made the wrong call when he had him give table 50 to Carmine, and was annoyed at Sabrina for taking table 55 when it should have been his, he knew she had worked hard for this table and was happy for her that she would probably be taken care of by her guests at this party.

Milo never found out how much the party tipped her, but he figured it was an average tip because if it had been a low tip, she would have been complaining about it to everyone who would listen, and if it was a great tip, she would have been bragging about it for the rest of the evening.

Milo was taking an order when he heard Sarah, who was waiting on the table behind him, talking to the guest. At first he wasn't paying attention to conversation, but he heard Sarah say, "Okay, let me go get a manager for you."

Sarah went over and got Victor, who came over to the table almost immediately. Milo turned around to help the table next to the table Victor was talking to. By now he was curious enough to hone in on what the guest was saying as she was talking to Victor.

"I ordered the Pastrami sandwich with no cheese," the older woman said, "and my friend here ordered the Rueben sandwich with no sauerkraut."

"Okay," Victor said, not quite understanding the problem because all Sarah told him was that the guest wanted to talk to her. "So what can I help you with?" Victor asked.

"Well," the woman said, pointing at the menu, "Right here is says there's a $1.49 charge for extra cheese, and here," she continued, moving her finger over, "It says there's a $1.99 charge for extra sauerkraut."

"Okay," Victor said, "But you didn't get any cheese or sauerkraut."

"That's my point," the lady said. "We did get any cheese or sauerkraut," but you charged us for it."

"We didn't charge you for it," Victor said. "It comes with the sandwich."

"But we didn't get it," the woman said. "If you charge more if someone wants extra, then it only follows that you should give a discount if someone wants something taken off of their sandwich."

Dumbfounded and not sure what to say, Victor looked at the check and said, "Okay ladies, I'll go adjust your check and be right back with it."

Another busy night and the restaurant was short-staffed. Amanda had closed the back row of tables and the prison cells, and was only seating the prison cells if they had a large party and if one of the servers was able to pick it up. Milo had all the high tops in front of the bar because Amy was the only bartender, as Amanda said, "They won't all get seated right away because people like the lower tables, but eventually they will fill up, and when they do, you'll be busier than you've ever been, so I need you to stay on the high-tops and not try to pick up the tables in the back section that I closed. A lot of the people who sit at the high-tops hang out longer because they are only having drinks and maybe an appetizer or two."

True to what Amanda had told Milo, most of the sections were full or starting to get full and Milo's tables were empty, because many people are reluctant to sit at a high-top, so he divided his time by running food and helping at the door.

"There are all these empty tables," one woman who Milo guessed to be only in her forties but a little bit of a curmudgeon, said to Caroline, pointing to the back of the restaurant, as Caroline put her name on the list. "Why can't we sit at one of them?"

"We don't have enough servers," Amanda said as she walked up to the host/hostess station. "We can't give you the best service possible if our servers have too many tables."

"Well why don't you just call in some of your backup staff?" the woman asked Amanda.

Not even knowing how to answer, and wondering if the woman really thought the restaurant had an unlimited supply of trained staff members just sitting at home, not working, waiting to be called in when needed, Amanda said "Is a high-top alright? Milo here is taking care of our guests at the high-tops tonight. He'd be glad to take good care of you. I can get you seated there right away and you can order anything at the high-tops that you can order at the other tables."

"Well if he can take care of us at the high-tops, why can't he take care of us at one of those tables?" the woman asked, pointing to the tables in the back of the restaurant.

"Ma'am," Amanda said, a little bit of frustration in her voice, not liking a guest telling her how to do her job, "I need my servers in their sections. The high tops will fill up eventually, so I can't have him running all over the restaurant taking tables."

Looking at her friend, the woman said "Whaddaya think?"

"Well, I prefer a table," the woman replied, as if a high-top wasn't a table, "but I guess it's better than waiting 35 to 45 minutes"

"Okay, I guess so," the woman said to Amanda.

"Milo will take you to one of the high-tops," Amanda said, handing two menus to Milo.

"C'mon with me," Milo said as he lead the women toward table 70. As they started to walk, both of the women and Milo noticed that Nathan had just cleared and cleaned table 52.

"What about that one?" the curmudgeony lady asked Milo as they walked.

"We still have a lot of people on the waitlist ahead of you," Milo replied.

"Okay," the woman grumbled, as they got to table 70, and Milo sat them.

"Can I start you with a drink while you look over the menu?" Milo asked. "A chardonnay or the Prisoner Red Blend?"

"Coke," the curmudgeony lady said. "Two of them, I think," she continued as she looked up at the other lady, who nodded in agreement.

"I'll be right back with your drinks," Milo said. "Do you want to start with an appetizer tonight? "We have a new appetizer," he continued. "Buffalo Cauliflower. Or our Cheasy to eat Cheese Bread?"

"Oh, that Buffalo Cauliflower sounds good," the other woman replied, looking at the table tent advertising the Buffalo Cauliflower. "Do you want to try that?"

"Sure," the curmudgeony woman replied.

"Okay," Milo said. "I'll put your Buffalo Cauliflower in and be right back with your drinks," and headed off to the bar area.

As Milo filled the drinks for the ladies, he turned around and saw Caroline followed by a party of three heading from the door toward table 52, and at the same time he noticed the women from table 70 get up and head toward table 52.

He wasn't sure what was said, but he saw Caroline and the party of three stop, one of the two women said something to her, and pointed to table 70, and then Caroline pointed to table 70.

At the same time, Milo noticed Dominic head to table 70 followed by two guys who Milo guessed to be his age or slightly older. Dominic seated the two guys and headed toward Milo.

"Bro," Dominic said. "I got someone who said they'd sit at a high top."

Milo looked back toward table 52, and as the two women headed back toward table 70, looking like dogs with their tails between their legs, Caroline sat the party of three at table 52. As the two women got to table 70, they noticed that their table had been seated during the time they got up to try attempt their hostile takeover of table 52.

"Whadda we do now?" the curmudgeony woman asked Milo, as Milo approached the table.

Milo guessed the woman were hoping he would offer them a lower table as "compensation," but he wasn't going to play that game, and it wasn't up to him to seat tables while they were on a wait. "How about the table right behind it?" Milo asked.

"I guess," the woman replied, and headed toward table 71, followed by Milo, Cokes in hand, inspecting the table, and then moving on to table 72, doing the same thing, and, finally settling on table 73.

As they sat down, Milo put their drinks on the table. "I'll bring your appetizer as soon as it's ready," Milo said, and headed over to greet the two guys at table 70.

"Hi guys," Milo said as he got to table 70. "How're you doing tonight?" he asked, realizing he had inadvertently changed up his normal greeting. "Can I start you with something to drink while you're looking over the menu?" deviating again from his normal greeting by not offering a drink by name."

"I'll try that Rustfield Red Lager," one of the guys said, looking at the other guy.

"I think I'll have the same," the other guy said, grabbing the table tent and looking at Milo, "This Buffalo Cauliflower... have you tried it yet?"

"Yeah, I have," Milo said, "It's really good."

"Better than the spinach and artichoke dip?" the guy asked.

"That's good too," Milo replied. "But the Buffalo Cauliflower is only here for a little while. You're better off to try that one while it's here."

"Let's start with an order of the Buffalo Cauliflower," the guy said.

"Sure thing," Milo said. "I'll be right back with your beers."

"Oh, and can we get a side of ranch with that?" the first guy asked.

As Milo grabbed his beers for table 70, he turned around and saw Carmine delivering an order of the Buffalo Cauliflower to table 70. As he dropped off the beers, he saw the ladies at table 73 waving him over. "I'll be right back guys," Milo said as he made his way to table 73.

"Why did they get their appetizer first when we ordered first?" the woman asked.

Realizing what had happened, Milo began to explain that that order was supposed to have been theirs, but because they switched tables, they caused the problem, but realizing the women wouldn't understand and figuring an explanation would probably only make things worse, he simply said "Let me go check on your appetizer," and headed back to the kitchen.

When Milo got back to the kitchen the second order of Buffalo Cauliflower had just been put up in the window.

"Mind if I grab these?" Milo asked Andy, who was working expo. "These two women..."

"Go for it," Andy said before Milo could even finish his question. "Amanda filled me in on those two women and she's been keeping an eye on them."

As Milo got back to table 73 he delivered the Buffalo Cauliflower to the two ladies. "I apologize," he said, figuring that saying anything else, especially trying to explain that their table-hopping is what caused the problem, would be in vain and would only make the situation worse. "Sometimes when two tables have the same order, the first order accidentally goes out to the wrong table."

"Well you need to tell the chef to make the first one ordered first," the curmudgeonly lady said.

"Of course," Milo said. "Are you ready to order your dinners?"

"How much sauce is on the Pomodoro Pasta?" the curmudgeonly lady asked?

"There's uhhh, um," Milo said as he was trying to think how to respond. "I think there's 8 ounces," he said not even sure if his guess was close or not. "But I can check if you'd like."

"No, that's okay," the curmudgeonly lady said. "Which is better," she continued, "the Pomodoro Pasta or the 8 ounce Sirloin?"

Not even knowing how to answer an apples-to-oranges question, Milo simply said "I really love them both but it depends what you're in the mood for."

"Oh," the woman said, putting her right hand up to her mouth with her index finger sticking out horizontally, moving her index finger up and down between her top lip and her bottom lip, as if that would help her think.

 "Okay, I'll have the Carnegie Salad with the dressing on the side," the lady replied.

"Wait. What?" He thought. "After all these questions about two completely different items, you're going to order a third completely different item?"

"But I do have a question," the woman added.

"Here we go," Milo thought.

"Do you think they could add croutons to the Carnegie Salad?"

"Sure," Milo said, relieved that ordering the salad wasn't going to be a process. "And what would you like?" he asked, turning to the other woman.

"I'll have the Roast Beef Sandwich and the split pea soup combo," the other woman said.

"I'm sorry," Milo said. "We only have the combos for lunch. We have the roast beef sandwich and we have the split pea soup but it would be a whole sandwich instead of just a half."

"But what am I going to do with the other half of the sandwich?" the woman asked, almost frantically.

"I can bring you a box," Milo said.

"Will it stay fresh?" The woman asked.

"I'll bring you a box that seals the air out," Milo said, thinking of the boxes they used for to-go orders instead of the boxes they used for guests who couldn't finish their food.

"Well I suppose…" the woman said "But tell the chef I want the roast beef medium, no pink and not burnt," she added.

"Absolutely," Milo said, knowing that all of their roast beef was pre-cooked, medium.

Turning away from the POS after ringing in a Carnegie Salad, a roast beef sandwich, and a split pea soup, Milo almost bumped into the curmudgeonly woman, who was standing right behind him.

"I want to change my order," she said.

"But of course you do," Milo thought.

"What would you like?" Milo said knowing that the Carnegie Salad would have been too easy.

"I think I'll have the Sweet and Sour Prawns and Pasta," the woman said. "It is good?"

"That's my favorite," Milo said, although he had never tried it.

"Okay," I'll take it, "and tell the chef to cancel my Carnegie Salad."

* * *

"Your card was declined," Milo heard from the table next to the table he was waiting on. "Do you have another card or cash?" Turning around, he saw Josh handing the card back to a gentleman at table 63 who was having dinner with three kids, in their late teens who appeared to be his sons.

His face turning red as Josh stood over him, the man reached for his wallet and fumbled to pull out another card. "Here, try this one," the man said handing Josh the other card.

As Milo turned from table 73, Josh turned from table 63, and Milo caught up with Josh as they walked. "Dude!" Milo said emphatically, "Don't ever say that to a guest. Everyone locks their card on their app nowadays, so next time that happens just ask them if they forgot to unlock their card. That way you won't embarrass them."

"But obviously his card wasn't locked," Josh said unapologetically, "Or else he would have unlocked it when I gave it back to him."

"Doesn't matter," Milo said, realizing Josh just didn't get it.

***

Wanting to greet the new guests at table 72, Milo tried not to make eye contact with table 70 as he approached the couple at his new table.

"How're you?" the lady said before Milo could even introduce himself.

"I'm good," Milo said, a little surprised. "How are you?"

"I'm great," She replied. "I'll have a glass of your Prisoner Cabernet Sauvignon."

"Uh, we have the Prisoner Red Blend," Milo replied.

"It says right here you have the Prisoner Cabernet Sauvignon," the lady said in a pleasant voice, pointing to the wine list on the menu.

A little embarrassed, Milo looked over at the menu where she was pointing and just said "Okay and wrote down Prisoner Cabernet Sauvignon on his pad, "And what would you like?" he said, turning to the guy with her.

"I'll have the "Boone's Farm Sunshine Pink Wine" the guy said.

Milo was not familiar with it but not wanting to make the same mistake twice, he started to write it down, when the woman, trying not to laugh, put her hand on his writing hand to stop him. "He's just playing with you," she said lifting her hand from his. "John," she said, turning to her husband, "Tell him what you'd really like."

"I'm sorry," he said to Milo with a little bit of a chuckle. "You seem like a nice guy. I just couldn't resist."

"No worries," Milo said. "I like a good joke," still not sure what Boones Farm was or if they even had it.

"I'll have a glass of the Prisoner Chardonnay," he said, "And I think we're ready to order he said, looking at his wife, who nodded in agreement. "Darling, what would you like?" he asked still looking at her.

"I'll have the 12 ounce Prime Rib, medium rare with a baked potato with all the toppings," she said. "With a side of ranch," she added.

"And I'll have the same thing, medium well. And a baked potato with all the toppings is fine," he said.

"Thanks," Milo said. "I'll put your order in and be right back with your drinks," googling Boones Farm before he rang in their drinks or food.

***

"Milo, what's up with table 34?" Belinda asked him, coming up from behind as he rang in table 72's order.

"I don't know," Milo replied. "I have the high tops tonight," turning toward Belinda.

"I know," Belinda said. "They got paged for their table and got seated at 34. They said Linus got them their drinks and appetizer and took their order while they were waiting for their table and pointed to you."

"Waiting for their table?" Milo said, looking at table 73 and seeing it was now empty, and glancing at table 34 and seeing the two women who had been sitting at table 73. "They had a table. In fact they had two different tables. I'll just transfer it to you."

"No, it's fine," Belinda said. "Just keep them. They know you… or at least they know Linus."

"Then I'll give you my next table." Milo said, not really wanting a table on the opposite side of the restaurant, and not really wanting these indecisive guests.

"No, it's fine. It really is," Belinda said. "I just got a party of 10 in the cell."

***

"How's the Buffalo Cauliflower?" Milo asked as he passed table 70 with the drinks for table 72. Taking a bite of the cauliflower, one of the guys gave him the thumbs up, and he continued to table 72.

"I've got your order in," he said to the couple as he placed their glasses of wine on the table. "Boone's Farm Sunshine Pink Wine and the Prisoner Cabernet," getting a chuckle out of both of them.

"Linus, you're alright," the man said. "I like a man who can take a good joke."

"Oh," Milo began, "It's Milo, not Linus," he continued realizing he had not introduced himself to the couple. "Those two women," he said, pointing to the now-empty table 73. "I think they misunderstood. And I've got your order in the kitchen too... two orders of the ground round with French fries and a side of bleu cheese," getting another chuckle out of the couple.

"How're we doing over here?" Milo asked as he got back to table 70."

"Great," one of the guys said. "I think we're just going to do a couple of appetizers, if that's alright," as if Milo had a say in what they ordered.

"Sure," Milo said. "What would you like?"

"We're going to have an order of the wings, all drums, extra crispy with extra ranch," he said, "And do you think they could put pizza sauce and pepperoni on this Cheasy to eat Cheese Bread, like a French bread pizza?"

"I don't see why not," Milo replied.

"Great," the guy said, adding, "with a side of ranch," as his friend put up two fingers in the shape of a peace sign, "make that two sides of ranch."

***

As Milo finished ringing in table 70's order, he turned from the POS at the bar and saw Sabrina delivering table 72's order. "Damn, that was fast he thought to himself," and then it hit him... "Oh shit, the ladies at table 73 moved to table 34 after I rang their food in. I need to go let Andy know."

Ready to make a beeline for the kitchen, he turned and heard "Excuse me."

He looked around and it was the lady sitting at the end of the bar drinking a glass of white wine next to the POS terminal. "Excuse me," she said again as Milo looked over at her. "What is that?" she asked, pointing to the two items Josh had just delivered to table 50.

Needing to get to the kitchen and not wanting to engage, but knowing he had to, he looked over at table 50 and then looked back at the guest. "The one on the left is the Fiery Prawns and Pasta and the one on the right is the Sweet and Sour Prawns and Pasta," Milo said.

"Which one do you like better?" the woman asked.

"Personally I like the Sweet and Sour Prawns," Milo said "But the Fiery Prawns and Pasta is more popular, but it's spicy."

"Oh," I like spicy the woman said in a sultry voice with a twinkle in her eye, Milo getting the feeling that she wasn't talking about food anymore.

"Then I would definitely recommend that one," Milo said.

"You got anything else spicy?" the woman asked, glancing at Milo's crotch, and looking back up again, with that same twinkle in her eye.

Now sure she wasn't talking about food, he took another look at her, guessing she was probably thirty five or so, and a little old for him, he pretended he thought they were still talking about food. "No, that's pretty much our only spicy dish," he said, wondering how he was going to get out of this conversation.

"Sup bro," Milo heard from behind him, knowing it could only be one person.

"Dominic, am I glad to see you, and I never thought I'd be thinking that." Milo thought to himself. As he turned around, he saw Dominic standing behind him with a Sweet and Sour Prawns and Pasta, a Roast Beef Sandwich and a Split Pea soup, and beyond Dominic, he could see the curmudgeonly lady standing at table 34 off in the distance waving at him.

"Bro," Dominic said. "Where does this go? There's no one at table 73."

"I'll take that," Milo said, taking the three items from Dominic, noticing that Dominic was now making eye contact with the lady at the bar, and the lady at the bar was now looking at Dominic with the same twinkle in her eye that she had when she was looking at Milo a few minutes ago.

"That boy sure can't find his way around," the curmudgeonly lady said to Milo as he arrived at table 34 and set their food down in front of them. "Don't you have numbers for the table or anything?"

"No," Milo said. "We put your name on the food instead of using table numbers and I forgot to tell him your name," making the split-second decision to risk a joke with someone who had been problematic since the minute she came in the restaurant, and, for a moment regretting that decision.

"But I never told you my…" the woman began, and then started to laugh, realizing he was joking, and reached out and put both her hands around Milo's right hand. "I think I like this young man," she said endearingly, still laughing a little looking at her friend.


Milo's sense of humor earned the restaurant a 3 star review.

**"There is a lot of confusion in this restaurant. They couldn't figure out why they couldn't give us one of the empty tables, gave our table away, then sent our appetizer to another table and then couldn't figure out where our entrees went. The food was delicious and our waiter Linus was a hoot and kept us laughing the whole time with his delightful sense of humor.**

**Bernice P.**

*** 

As the night wound down and there was only one table left in the restaurant, Milo and the other servers began working on their closing duties. There was a list of closing duties posted on the wall in the kitchen but everyone pretty much knew what needed to be done.

"Milo, I did the dessert station and I'm doing the soda station in the kitchen," Carmine said as she approached him at the soda station near the bar. "I may transfer table 35 to you. They're done eating but they're just talking now. All you have to do is cash them out and keep the tip."

"I'm not scheduled to close," Milo said, knowing that somehow he almost always ended up closing whether he was scheduled to or not, and he really didn't mind because that meant the other servers did most of the side work, and all he had to do was finish up a few loose ends.

"Puh-leeese, Milo," Carmine said, a little flirtatiously. "I have to be at my other job at 8 tomorrow morning."

Had it been Doris who asked for a favor in a flirtatious tone, he would have been right on it, but something about Carmine irked him. "Fine," Milo said realizing that it was almost closing time anyway, so while Carmine would get out perhaps a half hour or so earlier, it meant less side work for him. "Just make sure the ice and cups are stocked because I have to open tomorrow morning."

"Thanks hun," Carmine said to Milo knowing that there was no way she would have called him hun if he wasn't doing her a favor.

"Oh shit," Milo thought. "The mall condiments." Although they rarely used the mall tables, they put condiments on them every day, just in case, and unlike the tables inside the main part of the restaurant, they took the condiments off the mall tables and put them on a tray, and set them on one of the inside tables every night.

Milo grabbed a tray and headed out to the darkened mall to collect the condiments. Making his way out through the first sliding glass door, he set the tray on table 82.

"Hey," he heard.

Startled, Milo looked around, and saw Dominic leaning against the railing between tables 80 and 81, his butt on the top of the rail, his hands in his pockets, and his feet stretched out and crossed.

"Hey," Milo responded, not sure what else to say. "I just came out here to get the condiments," realizing he didn't owe Dominic an explanation, but grateful that those few words broke what could have been an awkward silence.

"Whatta ya doin, Bro" Dominic asked.

"I just told you. I came out here to…"

"After work," Dominic interrupted in a softer voice, taking his right hand out of his pocket and putting it on his upper thigh and moving it back and forth a little.

"No plans," Milo said, a little nervous, not sure why Dominic would be asking.

"Come grab a beer with me?" Dominic said in a questioning manner. "I've got a six-pack back at my place."

"Um, okay," Milo said a little tentatively but also a little excited. He had never spent time alone with anyone outside of a public environment, but getting more intrigued as the moments moved on, realizing what Dominic was probably insinuating. "What about you and Doris?" he added as he became more comfortable and started to take the condiments off of the tables."

"What about me and Doris?" Dominic asked Milo, his emphasis on the word "about," as he began to help Milo take the condiments off the tables. "She's a nice girl but we're just friends. What about YOU and Doris?"

"Um, same," Milo said. "We had dinner once after work, but that's it."

"So there you go," Dominic said. "But this is about you and me," he added. "Things are different between guys than they are between a girl and a guy. I like her but when things start to happen with a girl, feelings are involved. Not so much with guys."

"I'm down," Milo said, feeling as if maybe he was just being used, but knowing that the only guy he had ever felt an attraction to, had asked him over for a beer, and he knew he really, really, really wanted to be used.

Dominic's apartment was kind of what Milo had expected. Kind of messy, in an older building in a complex probably built in the 1990s, with clothes and mail, and plates and cups strewn all over the place. As they entered the apartment and the door closed, Dominic took Milo's chin between his thumb and his index finger, gave him a quick kiss on the lips, let go and went into the kitchen.

"Budweiser okay?" he asked.

"Uh, yeah, sure," Milo replied, not being much of a drinker. "So," he continued, trying to assess the situation and make conversation "You live here by yourself?"

"Nah," Dominic said. "I have roommates. You know one of them. Josh. He sleeps on the couch. Not the brightest crayon in the box, but a nice guy. And Joey. He sleeps on the air mattress in the bedroom and I have the bed in the bedroom. But we all do our own thing and no one really cares." He handed Milo a beer, sat on the couch, and patted the cushion next to him and said "Sit down. Relax."

"What if one of them comes in?" Milo asked as he sat down.

"We're just having a beer," Dominic said as he chuckled, Milo's hopes shattering for just a minute, "But we're adults and we all do what we want. Joey's girl spends the night with him all the time on the air mattress while I'm there, so I just roll over and try to ignore it."

"So you have people over often?" Milo asked.

"Every once in a while." Dominic said. "I kind of keep to myself. Me and Josh have been friends since middle school. We play video games a lot and we play together occasionally."

"Play --- together?" Milo asked hesitantly.

"You know what I mean," Dominic said with the same smile he gave Milo when he touched Milo in dry goods.

And it was then that Milo remembered - the touch in dry goods. It wasn't an accident!

"You're a lot more talkative tonight than you are at work," Milo said. "You never say much at work."

"That's my alter ego, my persona," Dominic said.

Not understanding exactly what he meant, Milo looked at Dominic quizzically.

"Keep the expectation low and they don't ask much of me. That way all I have to do is seat guests and sometimes run food," Dominic said.

"Well don't you want to do more than seat guests?" Milo asked.

"Of course I do," Dominic replied. "But not at Bubba's. I'm finishing my second year at Rustfield Community College working on a degree in genetic engineering. I have a GPA of 3.86. I've been accepted to six colleges, so I can pick from any one of them next year after I finish this semester."

"Well what about Josh?" Milo asked, trying to steer the conversation back to the here and now.

"Nah bro, he really is kind of dumb. It's not an act," Dominic said. "But he's a good guy."

"That's not what I meant. What if Josh comes home now?" Milo asked.

"Nothing he hasn't seen before," Dominic said. "But he won't come home. He went to his girl's place after work and once he goes there he's usually there for the night."

"His girl? Milo asked. "But what about you and him?"

"We're just friends and sometimes we play," Dominic said.

"So he's cheating on her with you?" Milo asked.

"It's not cheating if she knows," Dominic said.

"I guess," Milo said, never having really thought about the concept of tangled relationships before, still not sure if he agreed whether it was cheating or not.

"So what about you?" Dominic asked.

"I have a group of friends from high school, and we hang out, watch movies, play video games. But it's never one on one. My friends are mostly science geeks, kind of socially awkward. I mean I really like them, but sometimes I think they're clueless. I, uh, have never really been alone with anyone outside of a public place, not even as friends," Milo said.

"Yet you're here with me," Dominic said.

"You asked me to," Milo said.

"That doesn't mean you had to come," Dominic said.

"I wanted to come," Milo said.

Dominic leaned forward, put his beer down on the coffee table, turned toward Milo, and again put his thumb and index finger on Milo's chin, pulled Milo's face toward him, and kissed Milo again, this time not removing his lips from Milo's.

"So whadda you think?" Dominic asked.

"I think I want to go to the bedroom with you," Milo said.

***

Monday nights were weird. Because it was the day after the weekend, a lot of people didn't go out, and they were typically the slowest night of the week, so Andy scheduled just four servers, gave them five table sections, one server with five tables in each of the four corners of the restaurant, and didn't seat the rest of the tables unless he needed to, and one of the four servers had time to take an extra table. By spreading the servers out and having "closed" tables near each server's section, the additional tables they picked up if they had to would still be near their section, and usually were larger parties that often incorporated one of that server's tables into the larger party.

This was an unusually busy Monday night but things were going smoothly.

"Great job everybody," Andy said repeatedly as he passed a server when he walked around the restaurant, running food and bussing tables as necessary. "Keep up the great work everyone."

Milo had six tables because 34 and 35 were pushed together for an 8-top, and Caroline had seated table 26 with two adults who had four younger children and wanted to be seated "out of the way."

"Milo, your food is up for 34," Caroline said to him as she approached him as he was leaving table 45. "Eric is calling for a food runner and everyone else is busy. Want me to help you run it?"

"Yes please," Milo said. Milo had really come to like and admire Caroline because she was genuinely a nice person and somehow managed to control the door and help the servers out even though the latter was not specifically part of her job.

"I've got that," Milo said, as he and Caroline got to the kitchen and noticed Andy was starting to take the food for table 34.

"Here ya go Chief," Andy said handing the four dishes he had off to Milo.

"And I need those two Carnegie Salads, the Reuben without coleslaw and the Sweet and Sour Prawns and Pasta," Milo said to Caroline. "Do you think you can carry them all?"

"I think I can," Caroline said.

"Well just leave the Sweet and Sour Prawns and Pasta and I'll come back for it," Milo said.

***

"It was exhausting, trying to catch up on the work from the days I was away," one of the guests at table 34 said to another.

"Okay, here we go," Milo said trying to get the attention of the guests as he and Caroline got to the table, food in hand.

"Well were you able to get anyone else to help you?" the other guest asked.

"Not really," the first guest said. "They're cases I was working on, so I really had to do the work myself," the first guest replied.

"Okay, I've got the Fiery Prawns and Pasta," Milo said, trying to get someone's attention, he and Caroline still holding all the food.

"I had the Carnegie Salad with dressing on the side," another guest said.

"I had one of those too but I had my dressing on the salad," someone else said.

"She's got those for you," Milo said, motioning with his head to Caroline.

"I'm going to need some more dressing with my salad," the guest with the dressing on the side said, before Caroline could even put the salad on the table.

"I think I'll need more dressing too," the other guest with the Carnegie Salad said.

"Okay," Milo said, trying not to let his frustration show. "Who had the Fiery Prawns and Pasta?"

"Oh, me," someone else said. "That was mine," and Milo proceeded to put the Fiery Prawns and Pasta on the table.

"Uhhhh, that's not the Sweet and Sour Prawns and Pasta," the guest said.

"It's the Fiery Prawns and Pasta," Milo said.

"Well that's not mine," the guest who had the Sweet and Sour Prawns and Pasta said.

"Who had the Fiery Prawns and Pasta?

"I think that might be mine," someone else said.

"Might?" Milo thought, picking up the Fiery Prawns and Pasta and moving it in front of the other guest.

"We're going to need some more napkins," the guest with the Carnegie Salad with the dressing on the side said as Caroline put the salad down.

"And some more water," someone said. "We're all going to need a refill on our waters."

"Okay, I've got you," Milo said, still holding two Roast Beef Sandwiches on one arm.

"Sweet and Sour Prawns and Pasta," Sabrina said, walking up to the table with the last of the items the party had ordered.

"That's mine," the guest who had originally claimed the Fiery Prawns and Pasta said.

"And some more lemons," the guest who asked for more water said.

"I'm going to need some ranch for my fries," one of the guests whose food still had not been put on the table said. "Actually extra ranch."

"I've got you Milo said," figuring out who had the two roast beef sandwiches by process of deduction.

"I'll be right back with your dressings, waters, lemons, and napkins," Milo said, turning away from the table as fast as he could, afraid to even ask if they needed anything else.

\*\*\*

"I'm going to need more ranch," the guest who asked for ranch said as Milo got back to the table with a tray of dressings, lemons, and napkins and a pitcher of water.

"I need more Sweet 'N Low," the guest who asked for more lemons said, before Milo could even take anything off of his tray. "I don't like this stuff in the yellow packets."

"Can I have some HP?" one of the guests with the roast beef sandwich asked.

"Some what?" Milo asked as he began to take the items off of his tray and distribute them.

"Steak sauce," the guest replied.

"Uh, we have Heinz 57 and A.1." Milo said, having never heard of HP.

"I'd like the Heinz 57." The guest said.

Turning to get the additional items the guests had asked for, Milo grabbed the signed credit card receipt from table 25. He noticed the bill was $71.24 and instead of writing in the tip amount, the guest wrote "I can't math" on the line for the tip, and simply wrote $100.00 on the total with a note on the slip. "Those people at that table are assholes. You're a patient angel."

"It's things like this that make my job worth it," Milo thought to himself.

*** 

"How is everything here?" Milo asked as he got to table 26.

"Perfect," the mom said. "My steak is cooked perfectly."

"Great," Milo said, "And how's your food?" he asked looking at the kids.

"Mine's really good," one boy said.

"Mine's really good too," one girl said. "Are these really chicken toes?"

"Well we can pretend they are," Milo said.

"He's not our real daddy," another of the little girls said, pointing accusingly to the man across from their mother.

Turning red and bursting out laughing, trying not to spit out her food, the mother put her cupped hand up to her mouth. "This is my brother," she said, still chewing, looking at Milo. "Their dad is still at work."

***

"Folks, how're we doing," Milo heard Andy say, as he approached an elderly couple slowly making their way back to the cell.

"We're going to sit at that table," the woman said with a slight accent Milo couldn't make out, pointing to table 46.

Wanting to know what was going on, Milo went to table 45 and pretended to straighten and check the condiments, although he knew they were fine, so he could hear what was going on.

"Ma'am, we have a waiting list," Andy said, "We have people who were here before you who are waiting for tables."

"But we came here for dinner," the woman said indignantly. "This table is empty and we want to sit at it."

"I appreciate you choosing Bubba's, but all those people," Andy said, crouching a little bit and pointing toward the people waiting near the door, "also came here for dinner. It wouldn't be fair to them if I let you sit here before we got them tables."

"But there are all these empty tables," the woman argued.

"I've only got four servers tonight," Andy said. "We can't give you the best service possible if they have too many tables."

"Then get another server," the woman said.

"Ma'am, I uh, okay, just a minute," Andy said, knowing he was in a situation he would never win, turned around and tapped Milo on the shoulder.

"Walk with me," he said to Milo, not seating the couple but also not telling them they couldn't sit at the table. "Let them sit down but leave them alone until we get some more tables seated," he said to Milo as they walked toward the door. "It won't look good to the guests waiting at the door if you start taking care of them before we get the people who are waiting ahead of them seated."

"How many parties are waiting?" Andy said to Caroline as he approached the host/hostess station.

"Let them sit there," a man who was waiting for a table said, before Caroline could reply to Andy. "They're old. I can wait a few minutes more."

"My kids are getting restless and hungry," another man said. "Can we get a table too?"

"We have four parties waiting," Caroline said to Andy, looking at her tablet.

"I was just about to start seating more tables," Andy said to the guests who were waiting in front of him, although he had actually planned on waiting a few more minutes.

"I'm good for another table," Sabrina said as she walked by. "Or two. I have two tables who are done and paid and just camping."

"I'm good for another table too," Josh said.

"Okay," Andy said to Caroline. "Start paging people and have the servers wait here and have them bring the guests back to the tables themselves."

\*\*\*

"It's cold in here," the woman who sat herself at table 46 said, before Milo could even introduce himself.

"We just turned the air up," Milo said, knowing that no one had actually done anything of the kind.

"Up?" The woman asked. "It's freezing in here."

"Turning the air up makes it warmer," Milo explained.

"Oh. Good," the woman said. "I can feel it getting warmer."

Wanting to roll his eyes, Milo said "Well, my name is Milo and I'll be taking care..."

"I'll have a hot tea," the woman said, interrupting Milo. "What kinds of herbal tea do you have?"

"We just have black tea," Milo said.

"Just get hot water," her husband said. "Don't you have teabags in your purse?"

"I ran out," the woman said to her husband. "I only got three from that last restaurant we went to, oh, what was it called?" she asked herself, snapping her fingers to help herself think. "I used them last week. I guess I'll have the black tea," she said turning to Milo.

"Would you like sweetener with it?" Milo asked.

"No, I brought my own," the woman said, opening her purse and showing Milo and assortment of sweeteners in pink and yellow and blue and green packets, and a few in packets with colors he didn't know the name of. "But bring me an extra teabag... actually bring me some sweetener too."

"And what would you like to drink?" Milo asked the man.

"You got decaf?" the man asked.

"I can make you some," Milo said.

"Deal," the man said, as if they were negotiating.

"No one brought us any menus," the woman said. "You got any bread we can have while we're waiting?"

"One of our appetizers is the "Cheasy to Eat Cheesebread," Milo said, trying to convey the point that because it was an appetizer, there was a charge for it.

"Is it free?" The woman asked.

"No, it's one of our appetizers," Milo said.

"Oh well, bring it anyway," the woman said. "I'm starving. We had to wait a long time to get served. Does it come with butter?"

"No," Milo said. "It has cheese on it."

"Hence the name," he thought to himself.

"Oh no, no cheese," the woman said. "I can't do dairy."

"But you do want some butter?" Milo asked, not trying to call the woman out on her contradiction, but rather trying confirm what she wanted.

"Do you have oleo?" the woman asked.

"Oleo?" Milo replied, having no idea what oleo was. "I'm pretty sure we don't."

"Then just the bread, toasted with a big glob of butter," the woman said.

"Great," Milo said. "I'll have someone bring you some menus."


"How is everything?" Milo asked as he stopped by the mom with the three kids sharing the pizza at table 24, realizing he hadn't been there for a while.

"Oooohood," the mom said, putting her thumb up, as she was taking a bite of her pizza.

"I'm sorry," Milo said realizing that oooohood with the thumbs up translated to "good" for someone who was chewing on pizza. "I didn't mean to get you with your mouth full," although that was only partially true because Milo had figured out if you ask them how everything is while they are chewing, it makes it harder for them to ask for something else.

"No problem" the mom said once she had finished chewing. "Can we get a side of ranch... or actually two?" she added.

"Sure," Milo said. "I'll be right back with..."

"Oh, do you do anything for birthdays?" the mom interrupted.

Milo hated that question because they only did that for members of their loyalty club, and very few people were members because no one wanted to take the time to sign up. They just wanted something for free for saying it was their birthday, and the few times he had gotten a manager to buy them dessert "just this one time," it didn't increase his tip, and in fact often meant a lower tip because people who ask for something for free are likely to tip less than other people.

"Actually we do," Milo said, a twinkle coming over the mom's eyes. "If you're a member of Bubba's Prison Inmate Gang," you get a free dessert if you bring in the email you got or the card we mailed you."

"Bubba's Prison Inmate Gang?" the mom asked perplexed.

"It's just the name of our loyalty club," Milo said.

"Oh," the mom said looking disappointed. "I don't think we are. Just bring us the ranch."

Feeling a little bad for getting her hopes up, Milo added, "I can ask if the manager will buy you a dessert if you sign up online while you're here. It just takes a minute. All it asks for is your name, birthday, address, email and phone number."

"Oh," the mom said. "I don't think I have time to sign up right now."

"I'll be right back with your ranch," Milo said, knowing he had tried and that all she wanted was a free dessert, and didn't want to give anything in exchange for it.

***

"You know what I'm in the mood for?" the woman at table 46, now gnawing on a hunk of bread with a slab of butter on it said to Milo as she was chewing on the bread.

"What would you like?" Milo asked, noticing the unopened menus Caroline had brought over.

"Lasagna," the woman said. "You got lasagna?"

"Um, I'm sorry, we don't," Milo said a little perplexed that the woman was trying to order without even looking at the menu.

"Well whadda ya got that's good for us to share?" the woman asked.

"Uh, something like lasagna?" Milo asked, and not waiting for the woman to respond, added, "Well, we have our Basic Pomodoro Pasta. It's spaghetti with pom..."

"Whadda I wanna pay $8 for basic pasta for when I can make that at home for free?" the woman asked.

"$8?" Milo thought to himself. "This woman really hasn't looked at the menu. What does she think she's going to get for $8?"

"Well," Milo said. "Our sandwiches are pretty big. They're good for sharing."

"You got roast beef?" the woman asked.

"We do," Milo responded. "It comes on our brioche bun with melted Morbier cheese on top."

"Morbier cheese?" the woman asked.

"It's similar to Havarti," Milo explained.

"Ya got any Cheez-Whiz you can put on it instead of the morbid cheese?" the man asked.

"I'm sorry," Milo said. "We don't."

"We'll just take that with the morbid cheese," the woman said, "and tell the chef to put a lot of roast beef on it. We're going to share it."

***

"How're we doing over here?" Milo asked as he stopped by table 34, knowing he couldn't put off the foreboding task of checking on them, as he would be summoned to bring them something else, just by virtue of him being there.

"Go-od-od-nom-nom-nom-nom," one of the guest said chewing and shaking his head affirmatively, as the others joined in in shaking their heads affirmatively.

"Can we get some to-go boxes?" one of the guests asked, just finishing chewing.

"Sure," Milo said glad that this stop by the table was much easier than he anticipated. Anyone want to try the Duck My Diet I'll Try It Chocolate Cake or the I'll Regret It But Duck It I'm Gonna Get it Banana Split?" he asked.

"The what?" someone asked as a few of the other guests chuckled.

"Those're just the names of our desserts," Milo said. "It's just a chocolate cake, or a banana split. We also have an ice cream mundae... it's like an ice cream sundae."

Looking around, no one was taking him up on the offer. "I'll be right back with the boxes," he said.

***

"How is everything?" Milo asked, deciding to stop by table 46, noticing that someone had run the sandwich to the table, and the couple was now eating it, and also noticing the sugar caddy of sweeteners he had brought to the table was sitting on the table, now empty, and one teabag was in the woman's tea and another unopened teabag sitting on top of her purse.

"Delicious," the man said. "Do you cook the roast beef here in the restaurant?"

"Uh, I'm not sure," Milo said, knowing that the roast beef came in uniform bubble packs that one of the cooks cut open, and then dipped the roast beef in au jus sauce to heat up and add flavor."

"Well the chef sure got the temperature right on this one, and it's a great cut of beef," the man said.

"Perfect," Milo said.

"You were right," the woman said. "I think we're going to need a box. I can't finish this… unless you want to finish my half," she said looking at her husband. "This sandwich is huge."

"No," he said. "I can't finish my half either. "A box will be fine."

"So you saved room for dessert by not eating all your dinner?" Milo asked.

"We're stuffed," the woman said, as they both chuckled a little bit. "Just a box and the check, oh, and one more teabag."

\*\*\*

It was a typical Wednesday night and kind of slow. Andy usually scheduled four servers on Wednesday, as he did every other weeknight, and as he did this night. Sandy, who usually only worked mornings, had picked up a shift, and Sabrina called out.

"We'll be good," Andy said. "We'll give Kim the right front corner of the restaurant so she can pick up tables if the bar is slow, Doris is on to-go and can help Elizabeth on the door if she needs to, we have two managers here to help out, and we have strong servers," paused for a moment, and continued, "well, two strong servers and Josh."

The shift started off slow and by about 7 PM, each of the servers had had a total of four or five tables all night, and it had not been necessary to seat Kim, who had a slightly heavier than normal bar crowd for a Wednesday night.

"Are the PM shifts usually like this?" Sandy asked Milo, looking around and seeing that they each had two tables, and Josh, who was sitting back at table 76 texting on his phone, had three tables, all of whom were done and just lingering.

"Nah," Milo said. "This is slow even for a weeknight but the bar is busier than usual. Kim has a pretty good crowd. I think Andy will probably cut pretty soon."

"I'm going to start wrapping up dressings and wiping down the dessert station," Sandy said. "Maybe we can get out of here early tonight. You good if I break down the soda station in the kitchen and we can use just the soda station at the bar?"

"Absolutely," Milo said, both of them noticing that Elizabeth was seating table 45 in Sandy's section and Doris was helping a guest who had ordered a pizza to-go.

"You want that table?" Sandy asked.

"Sure," Milo said, grabbing some silverware and a rarely-used Bubba figurine, since it was slow and he had time to grab it, and headed off to table 45.

"Hi. My name is Milo and I'll be taking care of you tonight," Milo said as he approached the couple with a small child he figured to be about 4 or 5. "Can I start anyone off with anything to drink?" Milo asked as he got to the table. "A Long Island Iced tea, or a Greyhound?"

"You got Captain Morgan's?" The man asked.

"We do," Milo said.

"I'll have a Captain and Coke, short, with lime," the man said. "And you babe?" he asked turning to his wife. "The usual?"

"Yeah, that sounds good," she said.

"And she'll have a Screwdriver with Stoli," the man said.

Unsure what Stoli was, Milo looked at him, and then at her, "Um, I don't think we have Stoli," He said.

"Then Absolut is fine," the woman said. "Or Tito's. Anything is fine as long as it's not the well vodka. I have too much to do tomorrow to risk a hangover."

"Sure," Milo said, writing it down. "And for her?" he continued, looking at the child.

"Him," the woman said. "He'll just have a kid's Orange Fanta."

"Would you like to start with an appetizer while you're looking over the menu? The Buffalo Cauliflower is our new item," he said pointing to the table tent, "or the Cheasy to Eat Cheese Bread is great to share."

"Whadda ya think babe?" the man asked looking at his wife.

"I'll eat either," she replied. "You decide."

Unsure which to get, the Man looked at Milo. "Well the Buffalo Cauliflower is only here for about a month," Milo said, "so you ought to get that one while it's here."

"Sold!" the man said.

"And I think we're ready to order," the wife said.

"Sure," Milo said. "What would you like?"

"We'll both have the Sweet and Sour Prawns and Pasta," she said, looking at her husband, who nodded in agreement.

"And for him?" Milo asked, pointing to the child.

"He'll just have some of our pasta," the wife said.

As Milo got to the POS next to the bar, he saw the Doris accompanying a man with the to-go pizza to the bar area, look around, and seeing that all of the tables in front of the bar were empty, she said, "Feel free to sit at any one of those table you'd like."

"It's kind of lonely looking out there," the man said, looking at the bar and noticing the third seat from the right end was empty and the space on the bar in front of the seat had a dirty plate, and a rocks glass with the remains of a drink that appeared to be a Manhattan or a rum and coke or something with a dark liquor, with a few ice cubes that were melting. "I think I'll sit there," the man continued, pointing to the empty seat.

As he approached the seat, pizza in hand, the man put his pizza box on the bar, but unable to slide it all the way back because of the plate and glass, leaned over a little bit, pushed the plate and the glass to the left, in front of the man at the fourth seat from the end, pushed his pizza box back so the back end of the pizza box was even with the backside of the bar, climbed up on the seat, and opened his pizza box, the top part of the lid falling back and hanging into the bar.

"He changed his mind, and decided to eat here," Doris said to Milo, making air quotes as she said the words changed his mind.

As Milo continued ringing in the appetizer and drinks for table 45, Kim headed toward the right side of the bar to see what Milo had rung in and noticed the man with his pizza in a to-go box, looked at Doris with a "what-the-fuck" look, and Doris just shrugged apologetically.

"Whadda you need hun?" she asked Milo, pulling the chit from the service bar printer.

"We don't have Stoli?" Milo asked, "Do we?"

"Not anymore," Kim replied. "It was a big thing in the 80s. My parents used to drink it because drinking Stoli back then meant you had made it, but we stopped carrying it a long time ago."

As Milo made the kid's Orange Fanta, Kim finished making his drinks, and turned to go back to her bar guests.

"Can I get a glass of water?" both Kim and Milo heard the man eating his to-go pizza at the bar ask abruptly as Kim turned around. Too good to miss, Milo grabbed a tray, although he could easily carry 3 drinks without a tray, put the drinks on the tray, and meticulously arranged them.

"How much for a draft beer?" The man asked Kim as she set the water down.

"The Stella is $9 for one of our small beers," Kim replied "If you want something like Guinness it's $13."

"What about the light beers?" the man asked "How much are they?"

"The Bud Light on draft is $7," Kim replied.

"Ya know," the man said. I can buy a 6 pack of Bud Light at Kroger for $9.99 and you charge $7 for one beer. Just this water," the man said, pointing to his water, as Kim walked away, not having it and giving him the stare.

As Milo got back to table 45, he noticed Elizabeth and Doris seating several more tables throughout the restaurant.

As Milo went to greet his three new tables, he saw Sandy come back out of the kitchen to greet hers. "Well I guess I'm not going to get out of here early tonight, she said to him," as they both noticed several more parties standing at the front door waiting to be seated.

"You want one of my tables, since I have one of yours?" he asked her.

"No," she said. "Just keep table 45 and for the rest of the tables we'll just stay in our own sections. It's less confusing that way."

As Milo, Sandy and Josh greeted their new tables, Milo and Sandy with 3 new tables each, Josh with 2, and Kim, who still had a full bar with 1, Elizabeth began to take names, and some of the people waiting for tables went over to the bar, standing behind the seated bar guests to order drinks while they waited, unaware or not caring that they were simply increasing the wait time for themselves and the others by doing so.

"Andy said he'd be right out to help, but to see what I could help you with," Doris asked, as she approached Milo and Josh, Milo noting that although there were still several groups of people waiting at the door, there didn't seem to be many more people coming in.

"I'm good," Milo said. "I greeted my tables and they're all drinking sodas or waters. I'm going to go get them now."

"Can you grab my two Rustfield Red Lagers from the bar and take them to table 25 and tell them I'll be right back?" Sandy asked Doris as she walked up.

"Sure," Doris said, about to head toward the bar. "Want me to get their order if they're ready?" Doris asked.

"That would be great," Sandy said.

"Just don't ring in under to-go," Milo said, noticing Doris giving him the "of course not" grin.

"Uh, where do I find out how to make a Shirley Temple and an Arnold Palmer?" Josh asked.

"Come with me," Milo said, heading to the soda station at the bar.

"Um, are they real people?" Josh asked Milo as they headed to the soda station.

"Of course they are," Milo said. "They're sitting at your table. They want to eat. Of course they're real," Milo continued, wondering if Josh had been smoking something and unable to discern if his guests were real or not.

"Not them," Josh said. "I know they're real. Shirley Temple and Arnold Palmer."

"Uh, I guess so," Milo said, not sure why this was relevant now. "I think they were celebrities like from a hundred years ago."

"Oh," Josh said, "and the lady said to make the Shirley Temple with Ginger Ale, not Sprite."

"Okay," Milo said as they got to the soda station. "We don't have Ginger Ale on the soda tower, so you have to get a can from here," he continued as he squatted down to reach a can from the reach-in below.

"Wow" Milo heard "They're both like 100 years old," Josh said.

Looking up, Milo saw Josh on his phone. "Put your damn phone away and make the drinks," Milo said, standing up and handing the can of Ginger Ale to Josh. "Fill one of those glasses halfway with lemonade and fill it the rest of the way with iced tea." Milo continued as he prepared his own drinks. "That's your Arnold Palmer. And fill the other glass with Ginger Ale and put in a squirt of Grenadine and a cherry. That's your Shirley Temple."

"Wow, it sure got busy quickly," Milo heard from the bar. Looking up he saw the man eating his pizza out of the to-go box trying to engage Kim, who was uninterested and too busy to chat, in conversation. "At least I made it easy on you," the man continued, directed at Kim. "I got my own food. Oh, can I have some more water?"

"I greeted table 61," Andy said to Kim as he got to the bar. "I'm getting their drinks and told Elizabeth not to seat you. I don't think she realized how busy the bar was."

"Thanks Babe," Kim said to Andy as she refilled the pizza guy's water. "I'm almost caught up now."

"Okay," Milo said as he dropped the drinks off at table 33, the third of the three tables he got when he got triple sat. "Are we ready to order, or would you like some more time?" he asked, hoping they would want some more time, knowing he had two other table he had to get orders from.

"We're ready," the man said, but I have a question.

"So you're not ready," Milo thought to himself.

"What can I answer for you?" Milo asked.

"This roast beef sandwich, can I get it open faced on rye bread with the cheese melted on top, and mashed potatoes with gravy?" he asked.

"Um yeah," Milo said pensively, thinking as he spoke. "I don't see why we couldn't do it open faced, but we don't have gravy for the mashed potatoes."

"Well it says right here you have Au Jus. And you have pizza, which means you have flour, right? So just tell the chef to whip up some gravy. Pretty simple."

"Um sure," Milo said "I'll check and see," knowing that none of the cooks would be thrilled about making some gravy during a rush, when it wasn't even on the menu.

"And I'll have the Chicken Salad Platter," the woman said. "But I don't want the black olives. I don't want the cucumbers. I don't want the coleslaw or potato salad. I just want extra tomatoes and some green olives instead of the black olives."

"And for him?" Milo asked, looking at the child.

"Just the kids Mac "N Cheese," the mom said.

"Absolutely," Milo said, looking up and seeing table 35 waving him over.

"We were here first but you took their order first," the lady at table 35 said, as Milo got to the table.

"I'm sorry," Milo said. "Everyone came in about the same time, so I wasn't sure who got seated first."

"Okay," the lady said grimacing. "We'll we're ready to order. I'd like this pizza. I want the 20 inch pizza with pepperoni. Is that enough for the four of us?"

Milo hated this question because he didn't know how hungry they were. "It should be," he said. "That's a pretty big pizza." Normally he would have suggested a salad to go with it, but at this point he wanted to get the food into the kitchen as fast as he could.

"Okay. We'll just have that," she said. "Oh, and with a side of ranch," she added.

"Got it," Milo said, looking over at the other table, a party of two men, probably in their 50s, who had gotten seated at the same time, and were still looking at the menu, unable to tell if they were ready to order or not.

"Are we ready to order?" Milo asked, "Or did you want some more time?"

"We're waiting on two more people," one of the men said, as he studied the menu.

"Okay," Milo said, "I'll come back when they get here."

"No," the man said. "It's okay. I know what they want."

"Okay," Milo said. "What can I get you?"

"Well I'll have the Sweet and Sour Prawns and Pasta," the man said. "But can you tell them to make it spicy and leave the peppers out?"

"Sure," Milo said.

"And for the other people... they're on their way, they'd like..." the man put his menu down and looked as his text messages on his phone, having to unlock the phone in the process, "okay," he said slowly, reading the text messages. "Kevin would like the Reuben Sandwich, but he doesn't want a pumpernickel."

"Okay," Milo said. "What would he like instead? Wheat or a Brioche bun?

"Oh, I don't know," the man said, picking up his phone to text his friend. "And he doesn't want the fries either. He wants something else instead."

"He could get coleslaw, potato salad, or a baked potato," Milo replied, growing impatient, but trying not to show it.

As the man finished texting, Milo heard the chirp of an incoming text.

"Okay," the man said. "He wants wheat and a baked potato."

"Do you know what he wants on his baked potato?" Milo asked.

"Uh, no," the man said...

"How about if I bring him the baked potato and I bring him the toppings when he gets here?" Milo asked.

"Perfect," the man said, and looking back at his phone, he continued, "and Carlos would like the Meat Lovers Pizza, 16 inch," the man said.

"Um, we don't have a Meat Lovers Pizza," Milo said. "Does he just want pepperoni and sausage on it?" Milo asked, hearing the man's phone ring as he finished his question.

"This is him calling," the man said, answering the phone. "Carlos," he continued. "They don't have a Meat Lover's Pizza. Here, talk to the waiter," he continued, as he handed his phone to Milo.

"Hello," Milo said, taking the phone from the man. "I'm good. And you? We can put any meat on the pizza you want," and after a short pause, Milo continued "we have, um, pepperoni, sausage, ham, salami, ground beef," and after another pause he continued, "okay, got it," and handed the phone back to the man at the table.

Taking the phone back, the man said to Carlos "Okay, see you soon... what's that? Okay, I'll tell him. He wants two sides of ranch" the man added, hanging the phone up and now looking at Milo.

"And for you?" Milo asked, looking at the other man.

"What do you have that's keto?" he asked.

"Keto?" Milo asked, a little perplexed. "You mean gluten-free?"

"Uh, no, keto," the man said, trying to figure out how to describe it. "No carbs. When I was here last time you had a keto section on the menu, but I don't see it now."

"That was years ago," the other man interrupted. "Nobody has keto on their menu anymore. Now gluten-free is the big thing."

"Um," I'm not sure what has carbs and what doesn't," Milo replied, having never been asked that question before.

"Um, okay," the man said. "I'll have the wings. All flats, no sauce, and extra celery but no carrots."

"Ranch okay with that?" Milo asked innocently, knowing that almost everyone got ranch with the wings.

"No!" the man chirped. "Bleu cheese. Extra bleu cheese."

\*\*\*

As Milo finished ringing in the three orders at the POS at the bar, he noticed they were no longer on a wait, and that by the grace of god, he hadn't gotten any more tables. "Wow!" he thought to himself. "We went from being almost empty to about half full in less than 5 minutes," and then realized that this meant that the food would take longer to come out than if they had gradually gotten busy, since most of the food went into the kitchen at about the same time. Glancing through the restaurant, he saw that table 45 now had their food.

Making his way through Josh's section to check on table 45, he heard "excuse me." He looked down and saw a man at table 53 looking at his watch and then looking at Milo. "Can you please check on our food?" the man asked Milo. "We've been here 20 minutes, and" opening his hand and putting it out toward the table, he continued, "nothing. The restaurant's not even that busy."

Not sure if he should explain to the man that they went to from almost empty to half full in just a few minutes, Milo just said "Sure, let me go check," when Josh approached the table.

"Sir," Josh said. "Your order is almost ready. We've got the two pastas and the steak done. We've got them sitting under the heat lamp to keep them warm for you. Your pizza is almost done and I'll bring it all out as soon as your pizza is ready."

"What!" The man fumed, several guests at surrounding tables, and as far away as the bar looked over. "Our food is sitting under a heat lamp drying out while you're waiting on one more item?"

"Yes sir," Josh said innocently, not catching on that the man was furious. "We're keeping it nice and warm for you."

Having heard the man's outburst from the bar, Andy came rushing over.

"Sir, let me go check on what's going on, and I'll be right back," Andy said, "And I'll make sure to take good care of you."

As Andy headed back to the kitchen with Josh, Milo headed to check on table 45, who was now almost halfway done eating their meals. Trying not to make eye contact with any other tables, he couldn't help but notice the woman at table 35 waving him over again.

"Waiter," She said. "Can we get an order of those wings, with your medium sauce while we're waiting for our pizza?"

"Sure," Milo said. "I'll put them in for you right now. "Ranch okay with that?" he asked?

"Extra ranch," the woman said.

Finally able to get to table 45, neither the husband or wife even noticed him, Milo noticed that the Buffalo Cauliflower was almost finished and both were eating their pastas and their son was eating his Mac "N Cheese.

"I'm not sure how that happened" Milo thought to himself, impressed that somehow the Buffalo Cauliflower had come out first, followed by the pastas, in the right sequence, "But I'm glad it did."


"Everything good here?" he asked, both of them looking up and giving him the "It's great" nod.

Milo finally felt he was caught up, so he decided to go check on food for table 33. As he got to the kitchen, he saw an open faced roast beef sandwich with mashed potatoes and gravy and a chicken salad platter with lot of tomatoes and green olives. "That's mine," he said to himself, as he went to pull it out of the window.

"No more gravy," Ray said, as Milo pulled his food. "We don't have gravy. You think I have time stop what I'm doing and make gravy for one person when we're busy?"

"Sorry," Milo said, pulling his food. "I was gonna check with your after I typed that in but I got busy."

***

"Okay, I've got the chicken salad platter," Milo said as he got to table 33, "and the open faced roast beef sandwich," putting both items on the table. "Is there anything else I can get for either of you?" he asked.

"I think we're good," the woman said.

As Milo turned from the table, he saw Sandy walking with a pizza toward table 35.

"Okay," Sandy said, as she and Milo both arrived at table 35 at the same time. "I've got the pepperoni pizza," she continued, putting the pizza on the rack.

"Cancel the wings," the woman said to Milo. "They're taking too long. I wanted something quick while we were waiting on our pizza. We don't need them now that we have our pizza."

"Um, but, okay, I'll go let the kitchen know," Milo said, as he headed back to the kitchen, wondering if the woman really thought that wings that she ordered after she ordered her pizza would come out instantaneously just because they were an appetizer.

"How is everything?" Milo asked as he got back to table 33 to check on them.

"Well," the man said, putting both of his hands out toward his roast beef sandwich and opening his hands as he did so, as if to present the sandwich to Milo. "Look at it."

Not sure what the man was referring to or how to respond, Milo simply said "Okay?" trying to understand what the man was trying to convey.

Lifting up a corner of the roast beef, the man continued, "Look at this. There's hardly any roast beef on here" as if he expected there to be double the amount of roast beef on each half of the sandwich because he ordered it open-faced, "And the gravy… it's has no flavor. It tastes like Au Jus and flour and it's kind of lumpy."

"I'm sorry," Milo said, perplexed that the kitchen had modified his order exactly the way he requested and made gravy for him exactly as he had asked, and he didn't like it. "Would you like me to get you something else?"

"Don't you have just a regular roast beef sandwich with fries?" the man asked.

"You mean like the one on the menu that you chose to modify?" Milo thought to himself.

"We do," Milo said.

"I'll take that," the man said, handing Milo his plate. "And tell the chef they should take this one off of the menu."

"Crazy night," Doris said to Milo, as she was restocking the to-go items and he was finishing up his condiments.

"It was," he said.

"Dinner Diner?" She asked him.

"Sure," he said. "I may even get a drink this time."

*** 

"Two for dinner?" the hostess asked them as they walked into the diner.

"Yes please," Milo said.

"Follow me," she said, and led them to a table on the opposite side of the restaurant from where they sat last time they were there.

"Can we have that booth?" Doris asked, pointing to a booth directly across the aisle from the table where she was trying to seat them.

"Sure," the hostess said, as she turned and put the menus on the table. "Someone will be right with you."

Not sure which side to sit on, Milo looked at Doris. "You slide in first," she said, putting her hand out toward the right side of the booth.

"Well I guess that answers that," Milo thought, sliding into the booth, Doris sliding in after him, and immediately putting her hand on his left knee.

Not surprised this time and not minding it, Milo made every effort to act as if it was no big deal. He liked Doris and did not want to make her think he objected, so he picked up his menu and began to glance through the drinks.

"Hi. My name is Dominic and I'll be taking care of you tonight," Milo heard.

"Oh shit, this is awkward," Milo thought, looking up thinking maybe Dominic had a second job, not sure how to respond or even act. Relieved, he saw a kid he didn't recognize about his height and build with shoulder-length brown hair standing at the end of their table.

"Can I start you with anything to drink?" Dominic asked.

"I'll have this frozen Piña colada," Doris said.

"What is this Spiked Milkshake?" Milo asked.

"It's just a Mudslide," Dominic replied. "It's got uh…" Dominic opened his server book and looked at his cheat sheet. "Vodka, coffee liqueur, and Baileys Irish cream, topped with shaved chocolate chips."

"Is it good?" Milo asked, immediately hating himself for asking that question because he hated when people asked him that question.

"I'm only 19," Dominic replied, "so…"

"I'll have one," Milo said, cutting Dominic off.

"Can I please see your IDs?" Dominic asked awkwardly, giving Milo the feeling that he felt funny about carding people older than he was, but knew Dominic was just doing his job.

Doris removed her hand from Milo's knee to get her ID from her purse, and Milo pulled out his wallet and took out his ID, and they both handed them to Dominic, who examined them.

"Okay, thank you," Dominic said, handing their IDs back to them. "I'll go get your drinks now."

As Doris put her ID back in her purse and Milo put his back in his wallet, Milo felt her hand again, but this time it was on his upper thigh, not his knee.

"This is nice," Doris said.

"It is," Milo said awkwardly, not sure if she was referring to just being at the diner with him or her hand on his thigh. Unsure, what to say next to break what seemed to be an awkward silence, he looked at her, and added, "We're still just friends, right?"

As they both looked at each other, something came over both of them, and their faces moved closer to each other, and instinctively they kissed.

"We're still friends," Doris replied, repeating what Milo had said, but leaving the word "just" of her reply.

Feeling his heart beating faster than he had ever felt it beat before, he began to understand what Dominic, the other Dominic, had told him about feelings being involved when you're with a girl, but not so much when you're with a guy, although he really liked Doris as a person, but had never even really liked Dominic to begin with.

"Okay," Milo said. "I just don't want to do anything to hurt you."

"Hurt me?" Doris asked.

"Yeah, I mean," unsure what to say next, he continued, "I like you. The last person I uh, kissed," not yet wanting to reveal that there was a lot more than a kiss, "I didn't have feelings for, so it didn't matter. It matters with you."

"I like you too," Doris said. "If I didn't, I wouldn't be here with you and I certainly wouldn't have kissed you, and I wouldn't be doing this," she continued, moving her hand a little farther up Milo's thigh.

Noticing their drinks were now on the table, and not sure how or when they arrived, Milo took a sip of his.

"But that's just it," Milo said. "If anything more happens, I still want to be friends with you."

"We're both adults," Doris said. "If anything more happens, we'll still be friends."

As he listened to what Doris said, he began to understand what Dominic had said about feelings being involved with a woman, but not with another guy, but realized maybe it had nothing to do with gender of the other person and more to do with his genuine like and respect for Doris, something he didn't have for Dominic, at least not in the beginning. And he knew that taking it to the next level could sometimes change or ruin a friendship, and he certainly didn't want to lose Doris as a friend.

"Okay," Milo replied, taking her right hand in his left hand, still not sure if she was correct, but knowing he liked her. "How's your drink?" he asked.

Chuckling a little, she said "I haven't tried it yet, silly," as she took a big sip.

"Are you ready to order?" Dominic asked as he got back to the table.

Looking at each other, it became clear to both Doris and Milo that they weren't going to have food. "I think we're just going to have drinks," Milo said, pulling his credit card out of his wallet and handing it to Dominic.

"You down for another drink?" Doris asked. "Somewhere a little more private?"

"Sure," Milo said. "Where do you suggest?"

"My place," Doris said. "I have my own little apartment above my grandma's garage, and I've got some wine in the fridge."

"Perfect," Milo said.

Signing the credit card slip, Milo finished the last few drops of his drink, but noticed that Doris still had about most of her drink left. "You gonna finish that?" he asked.

Taking her drink in her left hand and taking a huge sip through the straw, she put her right hand back on Milo's left thigh, and began to move it back and forth a little bit.

"Okay, I'm ready," Doris said, as they both heard the slurp of the last little bit of Doris' drink go up through the straw.

"Uhm, Okay, I'm not," Milo said, taking her hand off of his thigh. "I'm going to need a few more minutes before I can stand up.

*** 

Doris' apartment was small but nice. There was a one-car garage with a staircase leading up to the apartment above the garage. It was two rooms, a living room-dining room-kitchen combo and a bedroom with a double doorway with no door, and, Milo assumed, a bathroom off of the bedroom. It was a little more frilly than Milo had envisioned, but nice.

"This is nice," Milo said. "Did you decorate it yourself?

"No," Doris said with a chuckle, opening a bottle of 2020 Salentein Malbec. "My grandma did. You like Malbec?" she asked Milo, holding up the bottle to show him.

"Um sure," Milo said. "To tell you the truth, I'm not much of a wine drinker, so I'm sure it'll be fine."

"Well, Malbec has got a little bit of a peppery finish, so if you don't like it, let me know."

"So, do you hang out with people from work very often?" Milo asked.

"No," Doris replied, handing Milo a glass of wine and taking one for herself as she sat down on the couch. "In fact almost never. Me and Sabrina did some day drinking once right after we started when we both got cut really early, but that's about it. Sit down," she said to him, seeing he was still standing.

As Milo sat down next to her she asked, "What about you?"

"Me and Dominic had some beers one night after work," Milo replied, realizing he may have gone where he didn't want to go with the conversation, just trying to make small talk.

"Dominic?" Doris asked surprised? "He never does much more than stand around and gawk at me," she continued, and all he can say to the guys is "Sup Bro" and to the girls is "Hey Chica."

"You'd be surprised," Milo said. "He has a lot more to say outside of work, and he's studying genetic engineering, or so he says.

"I think he really is," Doris replied. "I know he does really well at Rustfield Community College and I've seen him in a few of my classes. But I'm surprised he could carry on a conversation."

"So what made you invite me over?" Milo asked, trying to understand what Doris saw in him.

"Well, you're cute," Doris began as Milo began to blush a little. "But you seem like a genuinely nice guy. Not everyone is like that, especially not at Bubba's."

"Thanks," Milo said. "I think you're really beautiful," he continued. "And you seem like a really nice girl," his eyes locking with hers, their faces moving closer together as they had in the diner, and they kissed.

"You know," Doris said, motioning to the bed in the not-so-far off distance. "The bed is a lot more comfortable, and there's a lot more we can do in there," as she got up and walked toward the bedroom.

***

Milo hated working Sundays. It wasn't because he inherently hated working Sunday or had anything else to do on Sunday, but Saturday nights were one of the busiest nights, so a lot of the side work that was supposed to get done went by the wayside, and Victor often closed on Saturday nights, and Victor was the worst manager at checking the closing servers out, which compounded the issue of side work not getting done. Fortunately for Milo, Maria opened, getting there a half an hour before opening time, and Logan and Belinda came in right at opening time, so they had to face the repercussions of a shitty close more than Milo, who was the fourth server in, half an hour after opening. The bigger reason he hated working Sunday was the tips. Sundays always started off slower because a lot of people were in church, and got busy fast when people got out of church, and the people that came from church didn't have the reputation of being the best tippers.

"Sup Bro," Dominic said as Milo walked in for his shift.

"Sup," Milo said, as he looked around and saw that there were a handful of tables in the restaurant, a little busier than normal for this time of day on a Sunday

As Milo made his way toward the kitchen, he saw Maria making ramekins of dressings. "Shitty close last night," Maria said to Milo. "Nothing was restocked and there're no ramekins of dressing made. Belinda and I got the clean cups from dish, filled up the ice bins, made iced tea, and cut lemons. Logan's been back at table 76 texting or playing video games or whatever it is he does on his phone… said he's just waiting for a table."

"Figures," Milo said. "Who's the manager?"

"Victor again. He's a clopen, and he looks like he had a few… or more than a few drinks after work last night. He's in the office with his head on the counter."

"Well what do you need me to do?" Milo asked, clocking in.

"I've done most of it," Maria said. "I'm not sure all the silverware is rolled. Check that and start rolling if you can."

"On it," Milo said as he headed out to the dining room, noticing all three sliding glass doors to the mall were no wide open, Dominic pushing the mall tables together into one long table, with one round table on each end, table 87 being the only table not part of the conglomeration of tables.

"What's going on out here?" Milo asked Dominic as he walked out to the mall.

"Party of thirty," Dominic said. "One lady's here already and said the rest of the party is showing up soon. Victor said for you and Maria work the party together."

"Cool," Milo said, noticing a lone woman standing at the front door, looking over a menu, as he headed back to the kitchen, thinking she must here for the party of thirty.

"Party of thirty," Milo said to Maria, as he got back into the kitchen. "Victor said for you and me to work it together."

"Nice," Maria said. "I'll start making them waters. It's easier to put them out in advance with a party this big. Can you go put silverware out on the table?"

"Absolutely," Milo said, as he headed back out to the dining room, noticing the same woman still standing at the door.

"Are you here for the party of thirty?" Milo asked noticing that the woman was now holding the menu instead of looking at it and Dominic was now putting silverware out at each place setting.

"Yes, I am. That nice young man," the woman said, pointing to Dominic, "is setting that table up for me. It's my daughter's birthday. Will you be the one taking care of us today?"

"It will be me and Maria," Milo said. "Maria's in the kitchen making waters for everyone."

"Great," the woman said. "And what's your name?"

"Oh," Milo said, realizing he had not introduced himself. "I'm Milo."

"Nice to meet you Milo," the woman said. "I'll be paying for this, so the check goes to me."

"Nice and easy," Milo thought.

"They're on their way and I've got almost everyone's orders. They're texting them to me now. But I want to put some appetizers in so they'll be ready when everyone gets here."

"Sure," Milo said, looking at the menu the woman was holding. "Do you know which appetizers you want?"

"I think so," the woman said, moving over to the host/hostess station and opening the menu. As she opened the menu, Milo opened his server book, ready to write the order down.

"I think we'll do," the woman said, pausing for a minute, "Well let's do this. Let me get four orders of the Cheasy to Eat Cheese Breads," she said," as her phone dinged, a text coming through, and then another, "and, uh, one of each of these other appetizers," she continued, "uh but not the wings… they're too messy. So make it two orders of the Gotcha Nachos."

"Okay," Milo said. "And what toppings would you like on the Nachos?"

"Oh," the woman said, not realizing she got to choose. "How about just some ground beef, tomatoes, lettuce, sour cream, and cheese? Does that sound good?"

"It does," Milo said. "So, four orders of the Cheasy to Eat Cheesbread, one order of the spinach and artichoke dip, one order of the Cheese Twigs, and two orders of the Gotcha Nachos with ground beef, tomatoes, lettuce, sour cream, and cheese?"

"Ya know what?" the woman said, "Make it two orders of the spinach and artichoke dip and two orders of the Cheese Twigs. That way there's one for each end of the table."

"Your table's ready," Dominic said to the woman as he got back to the host/hostess station.

"I'll go put your appetizers in," Milo said, and when I'm done with that, Maria and I will bring all the waters out."

"Perfect," the lady said, "And when you get back out, I'll have all the other orders to give to you," as the ding of another text message came through her phone. "I've got them right here," she said, pointing to her phone.

As Milo and Maria finished putting out waters at all the seats, the woman said "I've got almost all of the orders," as the ding of another text coming through her phone.

"Great," Milo said. "I'll come back in a few minutes to get them from you."

"That last text message was the last order. Can we do it now?" the woman asked.

"Absolutely," Milo replied, as he took his server book from his apron and began to write.

As she scrolled through her texts, double checking them, Milo wrote the order down on his pad.

"Okay," Milo said once she had given him all the orders. "Let me read that back to you. So it's two of the large pizzas, those are the 20 inch pizzas, one with sausage and pepperoni, and one with spinach and artichokes, one Crispy Chicken Salad with two bowls, two orders of the meatloaf, one with fries and one with mashed potatoes, one Fiery Prawns and Pasta, two tuna salad sandwiches, both with fries, two plain burgers, both medium with fries, and one roast beef sandwich with fries. And the appetizers are already in the kitchen."

"Perfect," the woman said as she finished going back and forth through her texts to make sure she had given the order to Milo correctly and he had written it down correctly.

"I'll go put it in now," he said, noticing the guests were starting to come in.

"Thanks Milo," she said. Milo always liked when a guest called him by his name.

***

"Bro," I just seated that table," Dominic said to Milo, as Milo got back to the host/hostess station, pointing to the back corner of the restaurant... "Table, uh," he began as he looked at the table and tried to compare it to the floor plan on the tablet.

"65," Milo said.

"Uh yeah, 65" Dominic said. "Whose table is that?"

"I think that's mine," Milo said.

***

"Hi. My name is Milo and I'll be taking care of you today," Milo said to a woman and her two young daughters, noticing that the woman was flipping through the menu, back and forth, looking at the same pages over and over again. "Can I start you with something to drink while you're looking over the menu?"

"Where's the breakfast?" the woman asked Milo. "Eggs or something? I really want some scrambled eggs or an omelet, or something like that."

"I'm sorry," Milo said. We don't serve breakfast. We have the same menu all the time."
"Not even on a Sunday?" the woman asked. "Like a Sunday brunch, or something like that?"

"No, I'm sorry," Milo said. "We just have the one menu."

"Well do you have a breakfast buffet or something?" the woman asked, looking around the restaurant, as if Milo was hiding something from her.

"No," Milo said again, pointing to the menu she was holding," this is our only menu.

"Oh, well this is very disappointing," the woman said. "What kind of a restaurant is this that doesn't have a breakfast menu on Sunday? My daughters and I were really in the mood for eggs. Do you think the chef could make us some eggs?"

"We don't have any eggs in the building," Milo said.

"But it says right here," the woman said, pointing to the bottom of the menu, "that you have eggs."

Turning his head a little, Milo looked at the very bottom of the menu.

**Allergy Warning: Some menu items may contain or come into contact with wheat, eggs, nuts and milk. Ask our staff for more information.**

"That means you have eggs," the woman said.

"That means," Milo began, not believing that he had to explain this to a grown woman, "that some of our item may be made with eggs," the woman just looking at him, "before they get here. We don't have eggs here."

"Well what about pancakes, or waffles, or something like that?" the woman asked.

"I'm sorry," Milo said.

"Girls, what do you want to do?" the woman asked, turning to her daughters.

"I want to stay here" one of them said.

"Okay," the woman said. "I guess we'll stay here."

"Great," Milo said, not so sure it was great. "Can I start you with anything to drink while you're looking over the menu? A Bloody Mary, or a Long Island Iced Tea?"

"Do I look like I drink?" the lady belted at Milo.

"Um no," Milo said, "We also have Coke products, coffee, tea."

"I'll have a coffee," the woman said, black, with sugar. And girls, what would you like?

"I want an apple juice," one of the girls said.

"I want an orange juice," the other girl said.

"Great," Milo said. "I'll be back with those in just a minute, feeling as if this was a guest he really didn't want to wait on.

Turning around, Milo saw Logan standing in the opening between tables 43 and 45, staring at him.

"Dude, that's my table," Logan said aggressively. "I have the back half of the right side and you have the front half of the right side."

"Go for it," Milo said. "One coffee, an apple juice, and an orange juice."

* * *

As the guests got seated, the appetizers began to come up and he and Maria brought them out and distributed them throughout the table.

"So my name is Milo," he said loudly, so all of the guests could hear him, "and this is Maria," he said, pointing to Maria. "The two of us will be taking care of you today, and the rest of your orders are already in the kitchen.

Noticing table 50 had just been sat, Milo leaned over to Maria. "Can you see if they want any other drinks?" he asked her.

"Absolutely," she said to him, as he headed over to table 50.

"Hi, My name is Milo and I'll be taking care of you," Milo said to a putzy guy, a little overweight, who was bald on the top and had bushy hair around the side and back, he figured was probably a struggling playwright named Elliot and his two sons, probably teenagers, both a little on the heavy side, who looked like average kids now, although their hair was a little disheveled, and disheveled in a putzy way, not a cool way, who Milo figured would probably grow up to be putzy too. "Can I start you with anything to drink? A Long Island Iced Tea, or perhaps a Bloody Mary or a Coke or Sprite?"

"No, nothing to drink," the man said. "We'll have three waters with lemons."

And suddenly, the scenario played out in Milo's head:

*"And what are you going to do with the water?"*

*"Drink it,"* the man said.

*"And what do you call something you're going to drink?"* Milo asked.

*"A drink."*

*"Yet you just told me you wanted nothing to drink,"* Milo said.

"Sure," Milo said as his mind snapped back to reality. "I'll be right back with your drinks."

"Uh, young man," the putzy guy said to Milo, who was still standing there. "We're ready to order."

"Sure," Milo said. "What would you like?"

"I'll have the 8 ounce sirloin," the man said. "Medium well. Does it cost extra for the baked potato?"

"No," Milo said. "It comes with a baked potato, mashed potatoes, or fries."

"I'll have the baked potato," the man said. "Butter and sour cream… but put those on the side."

"Sure," Milo said. "And what would you like?" Milo asked, turning to the sons.

"I'll have the kid's Chicken Toes," one son said. "Can I get an extra side of ranch with it?"

"Sure," Milo said, thinking the kid looked a little old to be eating a kid's meal. "It's not a big portion," Milo added.

"He'll be fine," the father said.

"And I'll have the kid's Mac 'N Cheese…" the other kid began in a monotone voice.

"No!" the father said. "It says right here," he continued, pointing to the menu, "that is has yellow food coloring in it."

"Okay, then I'll have the kid's hot dog," the kid said in the same monotone voice.

"Sure thing," Milo said, thinking that the line about yellow food coloring in the Mac 'N Cheese was on the menu to be humorous and that there was probably food coloring in the hot dog, and the rest of the food they served, for that matter.

*** 

As Milo left table 50, he noticed Dominic had just seated table 52. "Perfect, timing, he thought."

"We're out of lemons," Milo said, setting three waters with limes at table 50. "Are limes okay?"

"Howduhyuh run out of lemons?" the man asked.

"Uh," Milo began, trying to figure out how to answer, but fortunately he didn't have to.

"Ya got any oranges?" the man asked.

"We do," Milo said, as the man stuck his fingers in each of the waters and picked the limes out of the waters and handed them back to Milo.

"Just bring us three slices of orange," the man said.

*** 

"And so it begins," Milo thought as he approached table 52, noticing the father in a blue oxford shirt with a beige blazer but no tie, the mom in a yellow dress, the young daughter, Milo figured to be between six and eight years old in a pink dress with a matching pink ribbon in her hair, and the boy, who Milo figured to be a year or two younger than his sister in a white shirt with a blue blazer.

"Hi," my name is Milo and I'll be taking care of you today," Milo began. "Can I start you with anything to drink?"

"Oh no," the mom said, chuckling slightly. "We don't drink alcohol."

"At least not in public," Milo thought to himself. "And when did I mention alcohol?"

"Do you still have the Guava Iced Tea?" the mom asked Milo.

"We do," Milo said.

"I'll have one of those," the mom replied.

"I think I'll have one of those too," the father replied. "And what would you like to drink, Mary-Catherine?" the father asked turning to his daughter.

"Apple juice," the little girl said in a mousy voice.

"And what would you like James?" the father asked his son.

"Chocolate Milk," the boy exclaimed, putting his arm up, his hand in a fist in superhero fashion.

"And I think we're ready to order," the mom said.

"Sure," Milo said. "What would you like?"

"This 20 inch pizza," the mom began, "Is it big enough for four people?"

"It is," Milo said, hating that question, but knowing that the 20 inch pizza was usually big enough for four adults, so it definitely would be big enough for two adults and two children. "You'll probably have leftovers."

"Well you think we should get the 16 inch pizza instead?" the mom asked."

"Um," Milo said, "It might be a little tight with the 16 inch pizza."

"Just get the bigger pizza," the husband said to the wife, "And we'll have leftovers."

"Okay," the wife said. "We'll have the 20 inch pizza with," and she began to look at the menu, "um, mushrooms, spinach, garlic…"

"Pepperoni," the son blurted out, putting his fist up the way he did when he said he wanted chocolate milk.

"Honey, are the kids going to eat spinach and mushrooms?" the man asked his wife.

"We can do half and half," Milo said.

"Okay," the wife said. "We'll do half with the mushrooms, spinach and garlic, and half with pepperoni."

As Milo turned away from table 52 to ring in their order, he noticed the restaurant was starting to get busier, and Dominic was seating table 51.

"Hi. My name is Milo…"

"Coke," the woman said, still looking down at the menu.

"Sprite," the man said, also looking down at the menu.

"Okay," Milo said. "I'll be right back with your drinks," neither one of them making eye contact with Milo.

***

"Dude, what's this?" Logan asked Milo, handing him two pieces of paper, as they both approached the beverage station. It was the first time Logan had spoken to Milo other than confronting him about a perceived injustice.

Looking at the first piece of paper, Milo began to read it:

**Visit Bubba's in Prison**
**Gift Certificate**
**Date Issued: 3/5/95**
**Amount: $7.50**
**Signed: Richard Whittaker, General Manager.**

The second piece of paper was similar:

**Visit Bubba's in Prison**
**Gift Certificate**
**Date Issued: 3/5/95**
**Amount: $15.00**
**Signed: Richard Whittaker, General Manager.**

But on the second piece of paper, the amount of $15.00 was crossed off and initialed. Next to it, someone had handwritten, obviously with a different pen, "$5.27 redeemed on 4/8/96 – spin dip – amount remaining $9.73 RW."

Both pieces of paper were wrinkled and all of the wording was pre-printed, except for the dates, amounts and signatures, which were all hand-written.

"Um," Milo said. "I'm not sure."

"I tried swiping them to check the balance, but neither one would swipe," Logan said.

"Well it says gift certificate at the top," Milo said, "So I guess they can pay for part of their meal with it. But I don't know what you do with it."

"But why wouldn't they just buy a gift card instead?" Logan asked.

"I don't know," Milo said. "You'd better ask Victor."

\*\*\*

As Milo turned around with the drinks for table 51, he noticed Maria dropping off the food at table 50. "Thanks," Milo said to Maria, drinks for table 51 still in hand, as he got to table 50.

"How's everything looking?" he asked.

"Is that all they get?" the putzy man asked, pointing to the meals in front of his sons.

"That's the portion size," Milo replied.

"Okay," the man grumbled. "They're growing boys. You'd think for the kind of money you charge here, the portions would be a lot bigger."

"How's your steak looking?" Milo asked.

"Great," the man said. "It looks great."

"Perfect," Milo said and he headed to table 51 to drop the sodas.

"Okay, I've got a Coke," Milo said, putting the Coke in front of the lady, "And a Sprite," putting the Sprite in front of the man.

"We're going to share the Carnegie Salad," the woman said before Milo could say anything else. "And bring an extra bowl," the woman continued. "And then we're going to share the Sweet and Sour Shrimp pasta. Bring an extra bowl for that too. But don't bring the pasta until we're done with the salad. We don't want it to get cold."

"Anything else?" Milo asked.

"That will be all," the woman said abruptly, dismissing Milo.

"How is everything?" Milo asked as he got back to table 50.

"Delicious," the man said, still chewing as he spoke, a fork in one hand and a steak knife in the other, and his napkin now tucked into his shirt in the shape of a diamond. "This steak is cooked perfectly. It's one of the best steaks I've had in a while."

"Great," Milo said, looking over at the man's sons. "How's your food?"

"Mine's good," one boy said.

"Mine's good too," the other boy said.

***

"Milo, your food is up for the party of 30," Victor said as he approached Milo who was heading into the kitchen. "Let's start running it."

As he and Maria both got to the kitchen, they started pulling the food from the window. "Can I get a follow?" Milo asked anyone who would listen.

"Sure," Belinda said, as she started pulling food, Victor behind her, and Dominic behind him.

As Milo approached the table, he saw something happen he had never seen before.

"Shhhhhhhh," the woman who was paying for the food announced to all the other guests. "Shhhhhh," she said again. "Our food is here so let's stop talking, take your phones off of the table, and move your arms from the table to make room for the plates, and let the servers give you your food."

"Shit," Milo thought. "I'll probably never see this again if I live to be 100."

***

"Anyone need anything else? Milo asked as the last few dishes were put on the table.

"A side of ranch," someone said.

"I'll take some too," someone else said.

"Me too," yet another person said.

"Tell you what," Milo said. "I'll just bring everyone a side of ranch, and when I get back, I'll start refilling your waters and sodas."

When Milo and Maria got back to the table, with five plates each with six ramekins of ranch, Logan was walking around with two water pitchers, one in each hand, refilling waters. "How is everything?" Logan asked as he refilled water.

"Great," a few people mumbled, as they began to eat their food.

Going up to the woman who was paying, and setting a few napkins down in front of her, Logan asked, "And how is everything ma'am?"

"Perfect," she said. "Just perfect."

* * *

As Milo dropped the pizza off at table 52, he noticed table 50 appeared to be done. "So is anyone ready for dessert?" he asked, as he cleared the empty plates of the two teen boys. Starting to pick up the putzy man's plate, he noticed the fork and knife were crossed, and about one quarter of the steak remained in the "V" between the knife and the fork.

"Oh, I'm sorry," Milo said. "I thought you were done."

"Ya know," the man said. "I really didn't enjoy this steak. It's overcooked and pretty tough. I could barely chew it. And there is all this grizzle," he continued, picking up his knife and moving it along the side of small remaining piece of the steak.

"Oh, I'm so sorry," Milo said as he looked at the side of the steak, not seeing any grizzle. "Would you like me to get you another steak that's cooked more to your liking with less grizzle?"

"No," the man said, sighing, to emphasize his disappointment. "We really don't have time and the boys are done eating. I really can't keep them waiting."

* * *

"Would anyone like any dessert?" Milo asked, as he and Maria cleared the last few plates from their 30-top.

Looking around, no one was taking him up on his offer, and the woman who was paying walked over to Milo and Maria. "Fantastic service," she said "Fantastic job by both of you. You can go ahead and just bring me the check."

"Thank you," Maria said.

"I really appreciate that," Milo said. "I'll be back with the check in just a moment."

"Here you go," the woman said, reaching in her purse and handing Milo a credit card. "Take this and run it through, and I'll give you a cash tip."

$497.90, processing, approved, and the credit card slips printed out.

"Fantastic service she said," Milo thought to himself as he walked back to the table with the credit card slips, the woman's credit card and pen. "Please give us a 25% tip," he thought. "Please give us a 25% tip... please give us a 25% tip."

As he got back to the table, Maria was chatting with the woman. "Okay, here you go," Milo said to the woman, putting the credit card slips, her credit card and the pen on the table, noticing that she had two twenty-dollar bills and a ten-dollar bill in one hand and two twenty-dollar bills and a ten-dollar bill in the other hand.

As she started to hand fifty dollars to Milo and fifty dollars to Maria, Logan walked up.

"How was everything this afternoon, ma'am?" Logan asked.

"Everything was fantastic Logan... it is Logan, isn't it?" she asked. "You're the young man who refilled our waters, aren't you?"

"Yes ma'am," Logan said. "That's me and yes, it is Logan."

"Well everything was just fantastic," she said again, pulling the ten-dollar bill from the money she was about to give Milo and the ten-dollar bill from the money she was about to give Maria and handing the two ten-dollar bills to Logan and handing two twenty-dollar bills to Milo and two twenty-dollar bills to Maria.

* * *

"Milo, your Carnegie Salad for table 52 is up," Tyler called from Expo.

"Okay, I'll be right there," Milo replied, as he waited while Victor did the comp for table 50's steak. "Can you grab me two chilled bowls?" Milo asked.

"Sure thing," Tyler said.

"Oh shit," Milo thought. I need to ring in their Sweet and Sour Shrimp Pasta so it's ready as they finish eating their salad."

"Can you please run that Carnegie Salad?" Milo asked Logan, noticing Logan leaning up against the side of the walk-in freezer where it met the counter next to the beverage station texting.

"Can't dude," Logan said. "Busy," as he continued on his phone.

"I'll run it for you," Belinda said, walking up, grabbing the salad, and heading out to table 51.

***

"How's the Carnegie Salad?" Milo asked table 51, noticing a couple, the man dressed in khakis and a yellow collared shirt and a blue blazer, and the woman dressed in a blue dress with a blue bow in her hair approaching table 52, following Dominic. The couple paused when they approached table 52.

"Fine," the woman said as abruptly as she had spoken when Milo took their order, again without making eye contact.

"Kathleen-Elizabeth!" the woman approaching table 52 said to the woman seated at table 52, who was now standing up, the two of them giving each other an air hug with a quick pat on the back. "How are you?

"I'm good," the woman who Milo now knew was named Kathleen-Elizabeth said.

"How are you?" Kathleen-Elizabeth asked the other woman.

"Great, just great," the other woman replied. "What did you think of the sermon this morning?"

"I thought it was so inspirational," Kathleen-Elizabeth replied. "It really made me reflect on our daily lives... oh, she said as an afterthought, you remember my husband William, don't you?"

"Yes, of course," the other woman replied, William now standing up and extending his hand to the woman standing at the table.

"And you remember my husband Matthew," the woman asked, as Matthew and William, and then Matthew and Kathleen-Elizabeth shook hands.

Standing there, Milo looked over at Dominic, who rolled his eyes, neither one of them sure if anyone actually remembered anyone else, or if it was just display of pleasantries.

"Well so good seeing you," the woman said, as Dominic lead them away to table 65.

"I think we're ready for a box," Kathleen-Elizabeth said to Milo.

"Sure," Milo said. "Did anyone save room for dessert? We've got…"

"Oh no," Kathleen-Elizabeth said, rubbing her belly. "I don't think any of us have room for anything else right now."

As Milo got back with the box and the check, and set them on the table, Logan was finishing up taking the order for table 65.

"We want to take care of their check too," Kathleen Elizabeth said to Milo, pointing to table 65, picking up the check Milo had just set on the table and handing it, along with her credit card, to Milo. "They are to do good, to be rich in good works, to be generous and ready to share," she said. "Timothy 6:17-18," she continued.

"Sure," Milo said. "I'll take care of that for you."

\*\*\*

"Hey," Milo said approaching Logan at the POS as Logan was finishing ringing in table 65's order. "My table 52 wants to take care of your table 65's check," handing Logan Kathleen-Elizabeth's credit card.

Logan looked over, gave Milo the "what-the-fuck-did-you-do" look, and took the credit card from Milo, and processed it, handing the card back to Milo along with the credit card receipt. "They'd better fucking tip me," Logan said, walking away.

\*\*\*

"Check please!" the woman at table 51 said to Milo as he was clearing table 50. "And a box."

"Absolutely," Milo said. Before getting the check for table 51, he stopped by table 52 to get his credit card receipt and Logan's credit card receipt. Both receipts were sitting next to each other, with a pen on top of each one, and a blue miniature bible placed neatly next to the pen on each check. Picking up the bibles to look at the credit card receipts, he looked at the tip on each receipt, both of which were strange amounts. Trying to figure out how the woman came up with these amounts, he studied the receipts for a minute, at first unable to figure out where these strange amounts came from. "Aha," he said to himself, as he looked at the total before tax on each slip, calculated 10% of each amount in his head, and divided the amount in half, and those amounts matched the amount of each tip.

In his short time at the restaurant, Milo had developed a thick skin for things like this, but Logan not so much. Thinking fast, Milo headed over to table 65.

"The family you were talking to over there," pointing to table 52, "bought your meal for you. All they asked was that you take care of your server, Logan."

"Oh, that's so sweet of them!" the woman said. "That's so nice! We'll definitely take care of Logan. Thank you so much for letting us know. If we want dessert, will Logan just start a new check for that?"

"Yes, he can take care of that," Milo said.

Grabbing a box and the check for table 51, Milo dropped them off. "Here you go," he said. "Here's the box and I'll leave this," he continued, "dropping the check on the table," whenever you're ready. Waiting for a response, he decided to head to the kitchen when neither the woman nor the man said a word.

***

"Here you go," Milo said when he found Logan in the kitchen on his phone, setting the credit card slip and the bible on the counter next to him.

"What the fuck is this?" Logan asked, picking up the bible. "What am I supposed to do with this? Pray that my rent gets paid, and what am I supposed to do with this?" he asked again, looking at the tip on the credit card receipt. "Buy new shoelaces?"

"They did the same thing to me," Milo said. "Shit happens. We have to take the bad with the good. But I stopped by your table and told them that my table had bought their meal, and all my table asked was that they take care of you, so you'll probably get tipped again... oh, and they're going to want dessert on a new check."

"Yeah," Logan said storming out of the kitchen, "Well this is your fault," as he tossed the bible in the garbage can and the credit card slip in his server book.

***

"Thank you, and have a great afternoon," Milo said to the stoic couple at table 51, as they got up to leave."

"Thank you," the man said, as the woman walked out in front of him. "Great service."

"I appreciate you," Milo said, a little surprised, to the man who had not said a word, at least not to him, the entire time they were in the restaurant.

Collecting the credit card slip from table 51, Milo saw table 65 waving him over.

"What can I help you with?" Milo asked.

"Can you tell our server we want a side of ranch when our food comes out?" the man asked. "We haven't seen him for a while."

"Absolutely," Milo said. "How is everything so far?" he asked, realizing it was a stupid question because all they had so far was drinks, trying get a sense of what Logan's tables thought of him.

"Everything's great so far," the man said.

"Perfect," Milo said. "I'll have him bring ranch with your food."

***

As Milo bussed tables 50, 51, and 52, he noticed Maria running table 65's food. As she left, Milo looked up and saw the man waving him over.

"I think she forgot our ranch," the man said to Milo.

"No problem," Milo said. "I'll be right back with it."

"Gullible is not a real word, Belinda said," as Milo entered the kitchen. "It's not even in the dictionary."

"Yes, it is," Milo said. "I'm sure it's a real word."

"It's not," Maria said. "People just use it all the time, but it's not real. Google it."

Milo pulled out his phone and opened his browser. "Oh shit," he thought seeing he still had porn hub open on the last window on his phone, quickly holding his phone down, so no one could see the screen, and opening a new window.

G-u-l-l-i-b-l-e, he typed in.

*Easily persuaded to believe something; credulous.*

*An attempt to persuade a gullible public to spend their money*

Turning his phone to show Belinda and Maria, they both started laughing as he held it up to them.

"So you are gullible," Belinda said.

"Belinda," Ray called from behind the line. "You're up. You're up twice."

"Want me to run table 30?" Milo asked, walking toward expo, closing out the browser where he googled gullible, and putting his phone in his pocket to grab the food.

"Sure Milo," Belinda said. "Thanks."

"Okay," Milo said as he got to table 30, "I've got the roast beef sandwich with fries and the kid's chicken toes."

"Roast beef sandwich goes here," the man said, "and the chicken toes goes to him," pointing to a little boy next to him.

"Chicken toes, chicken toes", the boy screamed enthusiastically, about his food being delivered, waving his arms in excitement, and hitting Milo in the thigh by mistake.

"Baby, keep doing that, keep doing that" a woman's voice suddenly screamed, from Milo's right front pocket.

The man looked up at Milo, shocked while his son looked up in an inquisitive manner.

"You like that?" A man's voice asked, also coming from Milo's pocket.

"Yeah," the woman's voice said. "You can do that all day."

His face turning bright red with embarrassment, Milo grabbed his phone through his pocket and pressed the silence button on the side as quickly as he could.

"What's he doing for her that she likes, daddy?" the son asked innocently.

"He's uhhh," the man began "He's uh, painting her house and he's doing a great job and she's really happy about it," the man continued, thinking quickly.

"I'm so sorry," Milo said, still red with embarrassment, not sure what to do or say next. "I am so, so sorry. I really am."

"Things happen," the man said, waving his hand over his son's head, as if to dismiss the incident. "It's okay. Not a clue," pointing to his son who was now eating, mouthing the words to Milo, Milo knowing that if it had been any one of the other almost 8 billion people in the world, he'd be looking for a job.

\*\*\*

"What..." Logan asked Milo, fuming, as he found Milo in the kitchen, "the fuck..." Logan continued, "is this?" he asked Milo, shoving a little maroon bible with a credit card slip for $8.64 and two one-dollar bills in Milo's face. "This is what table 65 left me and it's your fault."

\*\*\*

"Damn, that man from table 30 sure was fuming when he talked to Victor," Dominic said, finding Milo in the kitchen.

"What?" Milo asked, turning around, shocked and starting to turn red again and sweat, thinking he had dodged a bullet but now thinking maybe hadn't done so after all.

"He fucking ripped Victor a new asshole," Dominic said. "Victor said he'd address it with the server later, bought his meal and gave him a $100 gift card."

"Oh fuck," Milo said, sitting down on a milk crate, putting his head down into his cupped hands. "Fuck, fuck, fuck, fuck, fuck," Milo said.

"Bro, relax," Dominic said laughing. "You're so gullible. I'm kidding. Victor's been in the office hungover the entire time. That never happened."

Getting up, not sure whether to laugh or to cry, Milo gave Dominic a punch as Dominic blocked it with his hand, turning the punch into a handshake, laughing, which caused Milo to laugh.

"How did you even know?" Milo asked.

"Baby, keep doing that, keep doing that." Dominic said, laughing. "I was at the host station the whole time."

"Fuck you," Milo said now laughing, walking out of the kitchen.

*** 

There was a strange vibe this Wednesday night and at first Milo couldn't figure out what it was. Wednesdays were not typically particularly busy, and neither was this one. When he checked his sales they were pretty average for a weeknight, but the shift just wasn't flowing. And then he figured it out. Usually a weeknight shift started off slow, got busier around 6 o'clock or so and the restaurant got as busy as it was going to get by about 7 o'clock and then business tapered off by about 8 o'clock, but tonight pretty much everyone had come in between 6 o'clock and 6:15. Milo noticed Doris had a line at the to-go station, and Caroline and Elizabeth seating table after table, one in Milo's section, then one in Carmine's section, then one in Maria's section, then one in Josh's section, repeating the same pattern but skipping Josh on every other rotation, until Milo, Carmine, and Elizabeth each had seven to eight tables, and Josh had four tables. Everyone was doing a great job greeting tables and both Amanda and Victor were helping get drinks and once all the orders went into the kitchen in quick succession, the kitchen did a great job of pumping out the food.

"Dude," Josh said coming up to Milo at the POS at the bar. "This is bitchin'! I have four tables all at once. I'm gonna make bank tonight!"

"Great job," Milo said, not sure what else to say to Josh. "Keep up the good work."

As Josh headed back to the kitchen, Milo tried to consolidate in his head what he needed for each of his tables. He felt pretty good about having things under control, but something was gnawing at him. Turning around and doing a visual of the tables, Milo thought to himself. "The 8-top in the cell is chill… they're just eating. I dropped the check at 53 a while ago and they haven't put a payment out yet… I'm sure I dropped it but now I can't see it when I walk by the table. Table 55 is cool, they're done and I just brought them each another glass of wine. Table 65 is picking at the last few morsels of food on their plates and just chatting. I've dropped the check at table 54 quite a while ago, but they had not touched it and were still chatting. Table 64 is eating dessert. Table 76 is finishing up but they're taking their time, so I'll see if they want dessert. Then he remembered…. Damn, they wanted separate checks at table 76. Did I split that up for them?" he asked himself. Pulling the table up on Aloha, he was relieved to see that had already divided the check. "Perfect," he thought. "Okay, that makes seven tables and I'm sure I have eight." He pulled up the floor plan on Aloha and looked, and… "Oh shit, he thought! Table 85. I have table 85. I forgot I picked up a table in the mall."

Rushing out through the first sliding glass door, expecting the worst… perhaps they needed something and were furious that he hadn't been by, perhaps they were ready to pay, perhaps they had gotten up to look for him, he was relieved to see the young couple just casually chatting, laughing and smiling, picking at their food, having barely eaten half of it.

"How is everything?" Milo asked as approached the table.

"Amazing," the woman said, looking up at Milo. "Everything is amazing!"

"Perfect," Milo said.

"I hope we're not taking up your table too long," she added.

"Oh no," not at all, "take your time," Milo said, using his standard response to someone who hinted that they knew they were camping. When he had a four table section and they were on a wait, and someone was camping at his table just chatting for two hours, that's not what he really wanted to say, but tonight his section was big enough that if did get full, he wouldn't be able to handle it, and he was just relieved that they didn't think he had been neglecting them.

"Thanks," she said as Milo walked back to the rear sliding glass door and approached table 76.

"So is anyone interested in dessert?" Milo asked as he got to table 76.

Looking around at each other, no one took him up on dessert, and one woman said, "No, I think we're done. Just bring the checks please."

"Sure," Milo said "I've got them right here," as he pulled out his server book, opened it, and distributed the checks.

"I can get some of these plates out of the way for you," he said, reaching in toward the table, knowing the guests probably didn't care because they were getting ready to leave, but it would save him time later on.

As he leaned in to grab the first plate, people started handing him plates, and as they did, he stacked one plate on top of another. As he started to pick up the bottom plate, a few more people stacked plates on top of the pile Milo was holding, some still with silverware, and some with leftover pieces of food, until there was a stack of precariously balanced plates about two feet high still on the table in Milo's hands.

"Well it's too late now," Milo thought to himself. "I can't just leave them here, and if I let go, all the plates, dirty silverware and leftover food, will tumble onto the table."

Picking up the plates and trying to balance them as best he could, he leaned them against his chest, leaned back a little, and felt a little better about the integrity of the pile of plates.

"I'll be back shortly," Milo said, as he backed carefully away from the table with the plates still leaning up against his chest and slowly walking away from the table.

"Would you mind taking these plates for us?" the man at table 65 asked Milo as he passed their table, handing him two more plates.

"Um sure," Milo said hesitantly, squatting down just a little. "I can't grab them. But if you could you please set them on top, I can take them" he said.

"Happy to help," the man said, setting the two plates on top of the already-unstable stack Milo was carrying.

"We're ready to pay," the man at table 54 said to Milo as he passed by, holding out his check and a credit card. "Would you mind taking this from us?" he asked.

"Um sure," Milo said, sticking out his right thumb as the man slid his check and credit card into Milo's hand, Milo pressing the card between his thumb and the dirty plate at the bottom of the pile.

Glancing at table 53 as he walked by to see if they had put out money or a credit card, he still didn't see the check or any form of payment.

Trying to keep his eye on the entrance to the kitchen, Milo noticed the man at table 43 holding up his finger. Doing his best to avoid eye contact, the man kept waiving his finger until Milo could avoid the man no more.

"Waiter," he said. "We haven't seen our waiter for a while and we'd like dessert. What can you tell us about your desserts?" he asked.

"Um," Milo said thinking of his usual speech about their desserts and including the names of the desserts in his speech, usually evoking a laugh.

"Fuck it," he thought. "This asshole can see I have a stack of dirty plates." He doesn't get the speech."

"We have a chocolate cake, a banana split, and a mundae," Milo blurted out.

"What's a mundae?" the man asked.

"It's just our name for an ice cream sundae," Milo said.

"Do you have Toffee Bar Crunch ice cream?" the man asked.

"What the actual fuck?" Milo thought to himself. "This isn't fucking Ben & Jerry's."

"No, I'm sorry he said," feeling a plate shifting. "We have vanilla."

"Oh, just vanilla Ethel," the man said to his wife. "Okay, well then we're going to have to think about it," he said looking back at Milo, as if he was buying a car and Milo was a car salesman, and it was some kind of negotiation tactic, as Milo headed off to the kitchen to bring the plates to dish.

\*\*\*

"Young man," the man at table 53 said to Milo waving him over as he came back from the kitchen. "We've been waiting quite a while to pay."

"Okay," Milo said, looking at the table and still not seeing the check or a form of payment. "I can take it from you whenever you're ready."

"I'm ready," the man said.

Standing there, Milo wondered what to do next and what the man expected him to do. After a few moments, the man reached into his front right pocket, pulled out the folded check, unfolded it, put it on the table, looked at the amount, reached into his back right pocket, pulled out his wallet and then pulled a credit card partially out of one of the slits in his wallet, looked at it, pushed it back in, pulled another credit card partially out of his wallet, looked at it, pulled it the rest of the way out, picked the check up off the table, and handed the check and the credit card to Milo. "Here you go," the man said.

\*\*\*

As Milo dropped the credit card and the credit card receipts at table 53, a lady at table 76 put up her hand as if to say "We're ready for you." Milo headed over to table 76, hoping they had decided that just one person would pay, or at least that there would be a credit card sitting on top of each check. When he got to the table, everyone had their check laid out neatly in front of them, several with a one-hundred bill on top of the check, several with a fifty-dollar bill on top of the check, and one with a few twenty-dollar bills on top of the check. "We're going to need some change," the lady said.

\*\*\*

"Milo, I need to see you in the office," Andy said standing at the entrance to the kitchen as Milo walked in for his shift.

"Okay," Milo said, getting a knot in his stomach wondering what he had done, and following Andy into the kitchen. The walk from the entrance to the kitchen to the door to the office was only about 100 feet, if even that, but it felt like it was miles. The entire time Milo played in his head what he could have done that was so serious that Andy needed to see him in the office. He had never had a discussion with Andy in the office, except when they happened to be there by chance.

Was it about him and Dominic? Or him and Doris? But how would Andy know and what business of Andy's was it? Or was it about the burnt pizza at table 43 the other night? Why would Andy talk to him about that when it wasn't his fault? Was it the phone Porn Hub pocket incident? But that was weeks ago and the man said everything was fine and not to worry about it. Or the guest who called to complain about his to-go order, who Milo accidentally hung up on when he was trying to put him on hold to get a manager? That was an honest mistake.

He had walked between the entrance to the kitchen and the office many times, many times in one shift, as a matter of fact, but never did it seem to take as long as it was taking this time.

When Milo got to the office, Andy was sitting in the chair at the computer and Victor was sitting on another chair, which was turned backwards, his body slumped slightly forward, his arms folded, leaning on the back of the chair.

"Come in," Andy said. "Close the door."

Milo came in the office and closed the door, the knot in his stomach growing tighter and tighter.

"Have a seat," Victor said, pointing to a Cosco stepladder that was open. As Milo squeezed into the stepladder, the "seat" slightly tight, even for his relatively small frame, Andy began to talk.

"Milo," Andy said. "How long have you been working here?" he asked.

Nervous, Milo thought about it. "Um I think about six months," he replied, still not sure what the interrogation was about.

"It has been six months," Andy said. "And how do you feel about your job performance over the last six months?" he asked.

"Well, I don't know," Milo said, feeling as if he wanted to cry or just get out of the office and be somewhere else, anywhere else. "I guess I have been doing okay," Milo replied, trying to think what he could have possibly done to merit such an interrogation. "I mean, I try my best. I try to give every guest the best service I can. I try to help out, but I'm still learning," he continued, struggling to hold back tears.

"On a scale of one to ten, how would you rate your job performance here?" Victor asked.

"I don't know," Milo said "maybe a four or a five," he continued in a low voice noticing Andy and Victor just staring at him. "Maybe just a three?"

"Well that's not how we see it," Andy said, pulling out a piece of paper and moving toward Milo.

"I'm sorry," Milo said, bursting into tears. "I really tried. I really have," he said tears running down his face, as he tried to wipe them away with his curled right index finger, thinking about how much he loved working at Bubba's, but what had he done wrong and where he could get his next job?

"Milo, what's the matter?" Andy asked as he moved toward Milo, Victor getting up and handing Milo a box of tissues.

"I'm really trying my best," Milo said, still crying. "I really am. I'm so sorry," he continued, still not knowing what he had done wrong.

"Milo, it's okay, you're not in trouble," Andy said, putting his hand on the back of Milo's shoulder to comfort him. "You're really not in trouble. I'm sorry if I gave you the wrong impression."

Milo took another tissue from the box, and wiped his eyes.

"Take a minute," Andy said. "Do you want some water?"

"No, I'm fine," Milo said, starting to compose himself.

"Okay, I'm really sorry," Andy said. "I'm really sorry if I gave you the wrong impression. This is your six-month performance evaluation. I guess I should have explained that from the start. Take a minute to read this," handing Milo the piece of paper he was holding.

As Milo composed himself, still wiping tears from his eyes, he looked down at the piece of paper Andy had just handed him.

**"Employee Performance Evaluation."**

**General Performance: Exceeds expectations.**

**Guest Focus: Exceeds expectations.**

**Teamwork: Exceeds expectations.**

As Milo read it, his tears dissipated and a smile came to his face.

**Accuracy: Exceeds expectations.**

**Attitude: Exceeds expectations.**

**Overall Performance: Exceeds expectations.**

**Comments: Milo's performance has far exceeded our expectations. He is focused on the guest 100%, performs well under pressure when it's busy, and during the slow times, has a great attitude and is an asset to our team and motivates his teammates to do better by always doing the right thing.**

"I'm so sorry," Milo said, laughing. "When I saw the two of you in here and you began asking me questions, I thought I had done something wrong, and every little thing that ever happened since I've been here ran through my mind, and I couldn't figure out what in the world I had done wrong. I thought you were going to fire me, or at least write me up, and I couldn't figure out why."

"No Chief," Andy said "I'm the one who is sorry. I should have told you this was your performance evaluation and never should started off asking you questions like I did without telling you why you were here. You're one of our best employees and I'd never want to lose you."

"Thank you," Milo said, choking up a little. "Thank you. I really like working here."

"So what is your favorite part of the job?" Andy asked?

"The guests," Milo replied. "They can frustrate me, but I see a difficult guest with a difficult request or situation as a challenge to overcome."

"And what is your least favorite part of the job?" Andy asked.

"A side of ranch."

"Huh?" Andy asked, not quite understanding. "What do you mean?"

"A side of ranch," Milo said again. "Everyone wants a side of ranch with everything, and they never ask for it until after I'm at their table, holding their hot food trying to put it down while they continue their conversation. Some of the things that go on in this restaurant... I could write a book about it."

*** 

## How the Book Started

A lot of the interactions we see in the media between guests and servers or bartenders begin or end with a snappy or snarky lines with or to the guest. They make for great comedy, but this is not restaurant life, and not reality. If a server or bartender talked the way the characters on television shows and in the movies talked to guests, they would no longer be employed.

Like every industry, restaurant staff has its frustrations that only people who work in the industry understand. I wanted to write a book that shows the things that guests do, their odd requests, and the way these things affect servers and bartenders from the point of view of the servers and bartenders, and the way servers and bartenders really react and handle them, WITHOUT the snappy or snarky interactions.

Milo may seem like the unluckiest guy in the world, getting only the problem tables and the tables that ask silly questions, but I can assure you that Milo has had his fair share of easy, non-problematic tables where everything went fine, and the guests tipped him more than appropriately. But nobody wants to read about that.

Am I Milo? The quick answer is no, but in any story, there is a little bit of the author in the protagonist. Most of the situations in this book are based on real situations that anyone who has ever worked in a restaurant has experienced or at very least witnessed. Some are real.

## My Soapbox

Last, many people question if tipping is a good thing, and why they should tip. There is an argument that restaurants should pay their servers "a decent wage," because "it's the restaurant's responsibility to pay their servers. It's not the customer's responsibility to pay the restaurant's employees."

I understand part of the thought process behind this argument, but it's flawed. The truth is, that if restaurants paid their servers more, the price of food would go up. I've heard suggestions that restaurants could pay their servers more and tipping could be eliminated. The flaw with this suggestion is that if that was to happen, there would be a shortage of servers, because it would be almost impossible to pay servers what they can make in tips. The reason service in restaurants is *usually* good is that a server's income is based on the service they provide, as it is in any other industry where the employee is paid on commission or bonuses. Perhaps restaurants could pay their servers more without raising prices and simply reduce profits, but you could say that about any industry. Call it corporate greed, and it may be, but that's no reason to deny your server his or her income.

The argument that it's not the customer's responsibility to pay the restaurant's employees is simply inaccurate. It is that it is the customer's responsibility to pay the restaurant's employees. This is the way it works in ANY industry. If you buy a television, a car, groceries, or any consumer goods, go to the doctor, have your computer fixed, or use any consumer service, you're paying the company's employees when you buy that product or use that service. The difference is that the employee's pay is built into the price you pay, so you don't see it. When you buy goods or services, you are paying the company's employees indirectly, and the company pays the employees with the money you paid the company. When you go out to eat and tip your server, you are paying the company's employees directly. When you go out to eat, you the customer, have discretion as to how much you pay. When you buy other goods or use other services, you pay the posted price.

Use that discretion wisely and take care of the servers and bartenders who take care of you.

Made in the USA
Columbia, SC
24 August 2024

41084442R00096